A Candlelight Ecstasy Romance®

"YOU KNOW WHAT I THINK? YOU'RE STILL IN LOVE WITH JEFF."

Amy got very red in the face. Her lips parted, then shut. Finally she said, "You know that's not true, Nick. How could you even say such a thing?"

That hesitation, he thought, had been a fraction too long. "Because it's what I believe. If you love me, you'd marry me. It's either one way or the other."

"It's not just one way or the other, Nick. Not in this case. All I was saying was . . . I think we should wait a little while."

"In other words, no."

She stared at him, shaking her head, as if she didn't know him anymore. "I didn't say that. But now I *know* we should wait."

It was a gentle kiss-off, if he'd ever heard one. Nick couldn't stand to hear any more. He walked blindly out of the loft and shut the door.

CANDLELIGHT ECSTASY CLASSIC ROMANCES

A WIFE FOR RANSOM

Pat West

A CANDLELIGHT ECSTASY ROMANCE®

Published by
Dell Publishing Co., Inc.
1 Dag Hammarskjold Plaza
New York, New York 10017

Dell ® TM 681510, Dell Publishing Co., Inc.

Candlelight Ecstasy Romance®, 1,203,540, is a registered
trademark of Dell Publishing Co., Inc., New York, New York.

ISBN: 0-440-19684-1

Printed in the United States of America

December 1986

10 9 8 7 6 5 4 3 2 1

WFH

To Our Readers:

We have been delighted with your enthusiastic response to Candlelight Ecstasy Romances®, and we thank you for the interest you have shown in this exciting series.

In the upcoming months we will continue to present the distinctive sensuous love stories you have come to expect only from Ecstasy. We look forward to bringing you many more books from your favorite authors and also the very finest work from new authors of contemporary romantic fiction.

As always, we are striving to present the unique, absorbing love stories that you enjoy most—books that are more than ordinary romance. Your suggestions and comments are always welcome. Please write to us at the address below.

Sincerely,

The Editors
Candlelight Romances
1 Dag Hammarskjold Plaza
New York, New York 10017

A WIFE FOR
RANSOM

CHAPTER ONE

Nick Ransom's taxi sped along the expressway toward Logan Airport. Boston shimmered past him in the hot June sun.

It was all so routine he didn't look out; he was deep in the financial pages when the taxi swerved. Nick was thrown against the door.

A dark convertible almost sideswiped them.

"You nutty broad!" the cabbie shouted.

The convertible shot ahead. Nick did a double take.

The driver wore a wedding veil. It streamed back in the wind, revealing her glorious mahogany-colored hair.

This was a scene out of a wacky movie and Nick stared after the convertible, wondering what was up. The financial pages lay forgotten.

"Crazy female," the cabbie grumbled. "Nearly clobbered us." His tone blended relief and ire; his voice wobbled.

"Maybe she's late for the wedding," Nick suggested.

The cab was gaining on the car. What was she doing alone, dressed like that, racing along the expressway? Nick's curiosity was really aroused now. The taxi shot by the convertible and he got a look at her face.

It went with the hair—beautiful—but the expression was tense. For a second Nick's glance met hers. Her eyes were big, deep brown. Desperate-looking. A real runaway?

No, there had to be a gimmick. Life never imitated the movies, not for Nick Ransom.

Once again the convertible slid up beside the cab. When the woman's eyes met Nick's this time, her lightly tanned skin reddened. She looked away. With a fumbling motion she snatched at the little crown that held the veil and pulled it off her head. Gorgeous hair, Nick thought. It shone in the sun as if varnished. The set of her pretty, satin-covered shoulders was tense and tight.

Traffic abruptly quickened: she pulled in front of the cab with a dangerous maneuver—she was gutsy, all right—and hightailed it onto the landfill that used to be Noddle Island, now Logan International. She braked to a jerky stop just ahead of them. Nick's driver swore.

"Don't sweat it," Nick told him. "I'll get out here." He thrust a bill into the man's hand, hauled himself and his briefcase out, forgetting the newspaper. Horns blared; behind him somewhere a couple of men shouted.

Nick eyed the woman before he walked into the terminal; she was jamming a note under the folded windshield wipers, snatching up the veil and laying it over her arm. With the other hand she managed a heavy-looking bag, oblivious to the racket of the traffic behind her.

Nick slowed his step, held the terminal door open. "Can I help you?"

She gave him one quick look from those big, soft eyes, shook her head and dashed into the terminal. Nick followed, watching her progress. He was subliminally aware of people staring at the woman in the wedding gown. She rushed hell-for-leather into a ladies' room.

Nick consulted his watch. He still had some time before his flight, and he was determined to find out what happened next. Lurking by a bookstand he pretended to scan the covers, but he kept an eye on the ladies'-room door.

In no time at all she emerged and this new scene nearly knocked the breath out of him.

If her face and hair had been a turn-on, they were nothing compared to her legs and body. Those items were sensational, neither hidden by the long-skirted, easy-fitting pink suit. She looked more together now but her fine-boned face, with its generous, sweet mouth, was still tensed up. She hadn't noticed him, which was just as well. She might think he was some kind of creep following her.

Nick waited at a discreet distance, saw her hurry off to a ticket counter. The same airline as his.

Nick's flight flashed on the board.

Damn. He walked toward the boarding area with a crazy feeling of deprivation; it was just like leaving a movie right in the middle. An absorbing movie, with a main character who really grabbed you.

Then he saw, with a sensation of disbelief, that she was boarding his flight.

Amy Hill leaned back in her seat and closed her eyes; she was still shaking all over. She didn't know whether she was going to laugh or cry. She was inches from hysteria. Thank heavens the next seat was empty. She was in no mood for conversation.

She slowly let out her breath; her heartbeat was getting back to normal. This was the first peaceful minute since she'd run away. She was too numb right now to hurt, but not too numb to recognize what a spectacle she'd made of herself.

Like those nightmares of public nakedness: when that man in the cab had stared at her, then asked if he could help, Amy's whole body had burned with embarrassment. As if the wedding gown were poisoned, the way Medea had poisoned her rival's.

It might as well have been.

She was still close to hysteria, but she wasn't going to laugh. A tear escaped, and then another. Amy wiped her cheeks. She'd never know where that mad, sudden courage had come from, the courage that let her say "Excuse me" to Jeff's astounded uncle, and walk right out of the church, race back to the house for her honeymoon bag.

Any woman in her right mind, Amy knew, would have changed at the house. But she'd been so wild to get away she couldn't spare a minute. And now she felt drained, emotionally exhausted.

The tears were too heavy to be captured any longer. They crept through her lids, splashed over her cheeks and ran right down to her chin.

Luckily the flight wasn't crowded. It took Nick about forty seconds to change his seat to the best one in the house—across the aisle from hers.

For camouflage, he'd opened his briefcase for an apparent study of papers, studying her instead out of the corner of his eye.

At first he'd pegged her as a gorgeous ding-a-ling who didn't know her own mind, too flighty to go through her own wedding. That didn't compute, though, from his observations now: she was definitely a grownup woman and her expression was intelligent. He even liked her clothes and the way she carried herself; she had flair, not flash.

Nick saw some magazines on the seat next to her; the same ones they had in Ransom's art department. Trade journals, for professionals. An artist.

Nick couldn't believe what he was doing—writing a script like this about a perfect stranger. But what the hell, the whole thing had been like a movie, still was.

Her eyelids fluttered. She was crying.

He had to do something. His work-loaded life hadn't left him any time to develop a way with women, so all Nick knew was the direct approach.

He moved to the outside seat and leaned over.

"Excuse me. Is there anything I can do?"

She turned her head toward the window, startled and caught-out. Nick saw her fumble in her bag for tissues, mop her face. In half-profile, she shook her head.

Nick sensed she needed to be left alone. He moved back. She got up and, looking straight ahead, went in the direction of the washrooms.

On the edge of his vision, Nick caught her return: she looked prettier than ever. The crying, instead of wrecking her the way it did most women, had just made her eyes shinier, her skin pinker. But she didn't look at him or anyone. It was a back-off signal and he obeyed it. He was not going to risk being obnoxious.

She was reading one of the magazines now. When she sensed he was looking at her, she read with greater attention or looked out the window.

The Boston–Chicago flight had never seemed this long to Nick. He couldn't wait to see where she went when she got off the plane.

Where she *went*. He was thinking like some private eye and he had no business to be. He ought to get back to the office and get a head start on tomorrow. But nothing remotely like this had ever come his way, and if he didn't follow through he had a feeling he'd always regret it. He hadn't acted on impulse for twenty years and it was about time he did. Maybe it was the pushing-forty crazies. Even so he was up for a little cloak-and-dagger stuff tonight.

Outside O'Hare, Nick flagged the taxi behind hers, told him to follow.

"So what is this, a bust?" the driver demanded.

"You sure don't look like a cop. So what are you, Fed?"

"Not Fed, not local. I hope it *won't* be a bust."

Nick kept his eyes on the back of her pretty head; she hadn't noticed him, apparently. That wasn't too great for his morale, but a lucky break under the circumstances.

Her cab stopped in a commercial neighborhood, warehouses converted into lofts. That *did* spell artist.

The curious driver wished him luck, and let him out about a half-block away. A passing truck gave Nick some handy cover; he lurked again in a doorway across the street, hoping she wouldn't see him. He'd come across as a real creep if she recognized him.

But his luck still held. She was so intent on the loft building she hadn't seen anything else. For the first time, Nick saw her smile. The smile changed her face completely, making her sweet and human. The frozen remoteness was all gone. Nick's heart slammed against his rib cage.

He had to meet this woman.

She was looking up: Nick looked up, too, at the second floor. He saw a blond woman and a dog at the window. The woman looked flabbergasted. The dog, a cute, fuzzy little gray Scottie, was scrabbling at the closed window of an air-conditioned room. The woman in pink waved back.

"Mischief! Hello there!" She hurried into the building, loaded down on one side with the suitcase. It took all of Nick's control not to cross the street to help her.

He waited until she disappeared into the entrance and was out of sight before he walked away, smiling. Nick thought about the dog's frantic welcome-bark, how glad she was to see it. The way it was with him and his Dobies.

He knew her dog's name and didn't even know hers. That was a kick in the head. But he'd know soon if he had to turn Chicago upside down.

A lot of people owed him and it was time to call in his markers.

The minute Rhoda opened the door, Amy let her bag fall to the rug with a thump. Home at last. Mischief leaped right up into her arms, nuzzling her chin and neck, trembling with excitement.

"Honey, what's happened?" Rhoda Silver demanded. The Chicago years hadn't crisped her Southern drawl.

"I left him at the church, Rhoda." The hackneyed line revived Amy's hysteria. She burst into a sobbing giggle.

"Sit down," Rhoda ordered. "Do you want a drink?"

"No, I had one on the plane. Is there any coffee?"

Before the words were out of her mouth, Rhoda was gone and back with a steaming mug. Amy sprawled out on the couch, took the cup from Rhoda. Mischief jumped up and snuggled close. She stroked him, murmuring, "I'm here now, kiddo. Here to stay." She sipped coffee. It was reviving, dark and strong.

"Better?" Rhoda asked. Amy nodded. Her

16

friend was still standing, looking at her. "So? Are you going to tell me, or do I have to wait for the season to change?"

Rhoda's Confederate Yiddish intonation was suddenly so funny that Amy's hysteria surfaced again. She started giggling. Then the giggles became sobs and she was crying.

"Amy, I'm sorry. And *not* sorry. You know." Rhoda handed her tissues, waited until she mopped and blew.

She did know. Rhoda had been skeptical from the first. Amy remembered her expression when she said Jeff wanted to be married in Boston. "You were so right."

"Look," Rhoda said abruptly, "I'm going to get out of here. Give you some time to unwind."

Amy's protest was only polite. She craved some quiet time alone. Rhoda went into the bedroom and Amy heard her expeditious packing. She was soon back, dressed for the street, carrying a small bag with a dolphin pattern.

Amy observed her with affection: her short blond hair was like a sleek helmet, her movements dancer-quick. "You're great," Amy said.

"I'm fabulous. Take it easy. If you need me, call."

"I will." Amy got up and walked with her to the door, hugging her. "Thanks for everything—sitting Mischief and the loft, and all that."

"Nothing to it." Rhoda grinned and her blue eyes were warm. "Just remember what my favorite heroine said: 'Tomorrow's another day.'" She kissed Amy and went out.

Maybe so, Amy thought cynically, but the idea didn't help much now.

Mischief barked, looking up at her, then he jumped again into her arms. She held him close, caressing his warm little body. He had to be the best dog in the world, always there when she needed him.

"Okay. Bath time." She put him down and he trotted after her, waited expectantly while she filled the tub. One of his favorite things was sitting on the rim while she bathed.

When she was going to the bedroom Amy saw the suitcase, still on its side on the carpet. She'd be damned if she'd even unpack tonight; tomorrow was time enough to confront her disaster-clothes.

When she got into bed, Mischief curled up at her feet. She felt like a wrung-out washcloth, but she could sense his utter happiness; in her highly tuned state, that touched her almost painfully.

She was going to have to pull herself together tomorrow, pick up the abandoned pieces of her life. Right now she could hardly look ahead a day, though. The numbness was going and she was beginning to feel the hurt. Her thoughts drifted back to the beginning.

It was hard to believe she'd met Jeff Windom only two months ago, at her first exhibition. He'd looked like a Puritan Apollo, real "old Boston" with classic features, scornful gold brows that matched his twenty-four-karat hair.

When they were introduced, he demanded, *"You're* the sculptor?" He pronounced it "sculptah," which charmed her. "You don't look like one."

"What does one look like?" she'd countered, faintly nettled.

"Muscles and a beard, like Michelangelo. You look more like a Sargent." She had to laugh at that, admitting to herself that she probably did look old-fashioned. She was. She'd wanted to be a sculptor ever since she was ten years old and began to haunt the museums, looking for all the splendor lacking in her family's shabby apartment. Looking for the meaning beyond the hardness of her parents' life.

Jeff Windom, with his elegance and ease, had dazzled her; represented everything she had never had. And her sculptor's eye reacted to his physical splendor. He was an Anglo-Saxon rather than a Greek god.

When he asked her to go out with him, she inevitably accepted. Within a week, she'd fallen into his arms. It was the first time she had ever made love: her senses and emotions were so aroused that she forgot the things that bothered her about him —such as his bland assumption that his way of life was the only one. After three weeks he asked her to marry him and she accepted, to Rhoda's dismay. Rhoda begged her to wait awhile, to visit Jeff's family and "look them over."

But Amy was too dazzled to listen, even when Jeff backed down from his agreement about a quiet wedding and wrote her from Boston that he wanted to get married in the "family church."

19

Against her wishes, she agreed, and went to stay with the Windoms for a week before the wedding.

The house on Beacon Hill was all that she expected, and she was proud that her knowledge of art impressed even Jeff's stiff-necked mother. But the visit was no idyll: Jeff's mother maneuvered her into a wedding dress she didn't even like, and she positively disliked the family. They were either older Boston Brahmins or hard-eyed young sophisticates who joked about the wedding.

And only two nights before the ceremony Amy and Jeff had a sudden, bitter quarrel. He'd said something about Mischief's kennel.

"You expect me to keep my dog in a *kennel?*" she shouted.

"Well, of course," he drawled. "Windoms don't sleep with pets, darling." Like his sisters, Jeff considered animals as hunting tools. She should have known then it wasn't going to work, but she'd put the matter on hold. Jeff had been equally indifferent to the matter of her work, which had been her whole life until then. Like an inexperienced fool, she'd still almost gone to the altar.

Then that one remark she'd overheard had saved her—the spiteful, low-voiced comment from one of Jeff's chic cousins.

"The whole thing is hilarious. I never thought it would get *this* far. She's tough, I'll say that for her. I thought surely Aunt Hester would have driven her off by now."

Amy had heard another woman answer, "Well, my dear, of *course* she's stuck. She must be panting for his money. I always hoped he and Alexandra would team up, but she's so stubborn."

"He'll never get over Alexandra."

The malicious little dialogue capped it. It burst the last fragile bubble. Astonished, Amy knew she wasn't going to go through with the wedding.

She smiled at Jeff's uncle, who'd been appointed in the absence of her late father to give the bride away, and walked right out of the church, meeting the startled eyes of guests coming in.

Amy came back to the present, expelling a long, shaky breath. She wasn't going to cry anymore. But the ache, the sense of loss would still be there.

Jeff Windom had been a dream. A symbol.

A symbol, she repeated to herself with slow enlightenment. She'd fallen in love with an idea, a' tradition. Not a man. She looked at him now, and herself, with clearer eyes. He'd represented all the solidity, the permanence, that her own childhood had lacked. His family had lived in the same house for more than a hundred years. Hers had struggled to pay the rent on a shabby, crowded apartment.

She wondered why on earth she hadn't realized this before. Because Jeff had been her first lover, he had aroused her as a woman, hypnotized her senses, blinding her to the truth.

The Windom way of life, to her artist's mind, had meant permanence and beauty, the continuum of art itself. The permanence she craved, that had made her opt for sculpture rather than another form. Stone, metal, and marble were the most immortal of mortal objects; the Parthenon still stood.

She'd been so aloof from the world that she

hadn't known that Jeff, who looked like a prince, was least like one where it counted . . . in the heart.

Her insights calmed her, gave her new courage. No matter what her awakened body demanded—and it would, haunted by the magic of their encounters—she was going to put romance on hold. There was more, much more, to aspire to.

Tomorrow *was* another day, after all.

Amy woke to a shiny morning, realizing she'd had twelve straight hours of reviving sleep. Mischief was begging with a twitchy nose; his stance said "Breakfast time."

"It sure is." Amy grinned at him, pleased to be hungry herself. After they'd eaten she dressed and took him for a walk. The day was a real Chicago special, brisk and bright, cooled by breezes from the lake. It was still too early to start her business day so Amy came back home to linger over coffee. She felt better already as she looked around the kitchen with satisfaction. She'd put a lot of work into this place and it had been worth every ache and pain. A pale wood sculpture of a winging gull was silhouetted against a sunny window between sky-blue curtains with a faint cloud pattern. Amy squinted at the gull, freshly pleased.

It was good. It *flew*. She strolled around the big studio portion of the loft, looking at other works again. *She* was good. And she was going to have a life again, starting right this minute.

She loved her loft, Mischief, her work, her friends. She loved the sense of expectancy Chicago offered. A "raw" city, of course, by the ethnocentric Windom standards. Well, damn the Windoms. Amy felt as if she'd been mad for a time and was sane again. Damn the Windoms, maybe. But not Jeff. Not yet. She felt a little pull at her heart, looking at the ring. It symbolized the death of a dream.

But she had to face the hardest part of the day—getting the ring ready to mail. She got to it. Handling rare objects so often in the museum, she made short work of the careful packaging, putting the car keys in a separate envelope.

The next chore was the wedding gown and veil: they'd have to be cleaned before they were shipped back to Mrs. Windom. With a sense of utter unreality Amy zipped the items into a giant garment bag.

The doorbell made her jump, her pulse hammer. A telegram from Jeff? Impossible. After what she'd pulled, he'd never approach her again. Amy spoke into the intercom; it was a delivery man from a well-known service.

Puzzled, Amy admitted him and signed for the parcel. When she unwrapped it, a slick black box revealed itself. On the box was the golden logo of Chicago's Oz Boutique, an "animal boutique" so snobby and expensive Amy had never set foot in it. If there was one thing she loathed, it was pet owners who tried to make their animals as high-toned as they were.

It had to be a mistake. She looked at the wrapping again. No. There was her name and address, as plain as her own nose. Curious, she opened the box.

Inside were a dog collar and leash of glove-soft, bright pink leather, elegant beyond belief. The color of her favorite suit. The whole thing mystified her. She couldn't imagine who could have sent the gift—not Rhoda, who made as much fun of the Oz as Amy did. And certainly not Jeff; he was no animal lover. But the collar and leash were undeniably beautiful. There was no point in trying to return them. No card was enclosed.

She put the new collar and leash on Mischief and admitted they looked grand on his shaggy gray coat. He seemed to like his new accessories: he pranced and preened, comfortable in the butter-soft collar.

As she went about her errands Amy was still wondering who could have sent the package. But she forgot about it when she walked into the specialty cleaners and the man opened the garment bag.

She thought for one horrible second that he was going to ask her if she'd "changed her mind." Instead he murmured politely, "Exquisite."

Amy blurted, "Isn't it? It's a costume for a play." Now she felt silly, offering the unasked-for information. The cleaner eyed her: theatrical and opera costumes surrounded him. They were probably brought in only by wardrobe people, and Amy would bet he knew every one of them. She blushed. Taking her ticket, she fled.

In the line at the post office Amy noticed a man ahead of her with blond hair like Jeff's; she felt a

24

small dart of pain, of new humiliation. It was going to take a lot longer than a day before she started to heal.

Amy took Mischief for a long walk, more for her sake than his. She needed to clear her head. She was going to have to give herself a little mourning time, maybe. But that hadn't worked with her mother's death; keeping busy had. Maybe it was time to think about getting back to work.

But she was chilled by the idea of people finding out what she had done; they might feel that anyone with so little judgment might be a poor risk as an employee. Still, she had to follow through; she hadn't gotten where she was by giving up before she started.

Back home she checked on the competition, stricken to learn that it was too late to enter. There were still the ads in the journal, colleagues to call advising that she was available. Not her co-workers at the museum, though; she didn't have the nerve for *that* today. Amy recalled the shower they'd given her. Good heavens, maybe she'd have to return the shower gifts, too.

But that was such a dismal notion that she thrust it aside for the moment.

The first thing to do was to go see Langella, her former instructor and mentor. Before she could get cold feet she dialed his atelier and was referred to the city gallery. Amy was glad to be spared the trip to his sprawling suburban studio, and she decided to pay a visit to the gallery. Snapping on Mischief's leash, she realized she'd absentmindedly put on the peony-colored matching suit.

She and Mischief would look like something out of a musical comedy in their ensembles, but what the hell, she concluded. She needed all the brightness she could get today. They taxied to the Langella Gallery on the lakefront. As soon as she entered its white, light-flooded interior, Amy's spirits began to rise.

"Amy!" Sam Langella shouted across the echoing space. "What are you doing in *Chicago?*" His assistants, in the midst of placing a new piece, stood by respectfully, eyeing Amy. They were students she didn't know, but their manner soothed her ego; it was obvious they knew her work and admired it.

Awe was generally the first emotion Sam aroused in people. He was one of the best sculptors in America, and he'd taught Amy all that was worth knowing. As usual he was dressed like a stonemason coming back from the quarry, plastery and rumpled. Even his mane of graying hair was dusty—it looked like Mischief's, Amy thought with fond amusement. The Scottie was dancing toward Langella, who petted him with the jocular roughness he loved.

Langella's massive arms and trim, stocky physique contradicted his fifty-five years; his black eyes were blade-sharp yet they had the unfocused look of those with creative intelligence. Right now his tanned, seamed face, with its pointed features, was broadly smiling.

Amy grinned back, but she could feel embarrassed heat waves under her skin. She could hardly answer his question here. "Do you have a minute, after you're through?"

"I have a minute *now.*" Langella said amiably to his aides, "You guys take five." He started to grab Amy's elbow with his big, dusty hand and drew back. "I need to be vacuumed," he joked. "And you're all prettied up." He gave her another penetrating glance. "Come on, let's go to the office."

He said nothing more until he'd closed the door on his paradoxical sanctum, a place that reflected his complex temperament. Beautiful art objects rubbed shoulders with stained tools and untidy periodicals; behind his handsome desk was a cockeyed, comfortable old chair.

"Okay," he said in his deep, gravelly baritone. "Sit. And tell me."

She told him, in excruciating detail, while Mischief sat politely by her chair.

Impassively Langella nodded. "I thought it was something like that. I'm glad, Amy. I never liked that guy, as you well know." She certainly did know. Langella had been even less enthusiastic than Rhoda. It astonished her now that the judgment of two people she loved and respected had counted for so little.

"Neither did Marta," she murmured. Langella's good-looking Scandinavian wife had obviously shared her husband's opinion.

"Well, it took guts to do what you did, Amy." Langella grinned. "I always knew you had 'em." He laughed softly. "I'd give a lot to have seen it." Langella sobered. "Better now than later. Look,

I'm sorry. I know this has its very unfunny side. How are you feeling?"

"I'm feeling fine," Amy said firmly, beginning to mean it more and more. Talking with Langella was another kind of coming home. "And I want to get to work."

"That's the way I like to hear you talk."

"You know of any art-related jobs I can apply for?"

"Related!" Langella frowned. "You're taking the wrong tack. You'll never be treated like a pro unless you act like one, Amy. Stop dancing around the edges; get right in the center. You're one of the best. Just take that portfolio and march into the big corporations' art departments. Aim for a commission that means something. You know you'll get an A-one review from me. As a matter of fact, we had a lot of inquiries early this morning from a lot of people about your work. One guy was practically drooling. Bettina's got them all on record outside."

By the time she left the gallery Amy felt a hundred percent better. She was within walking distance of Rhoda's store, and it was about lunchtime. It would be great to see her, tell her everything that had happened in one short morning.

They arranged to meet at a sidewalk café where Amy could bring Mischief. He sat like a gentleman at Amy's feet, begging quietly from time to time, to the pleasure of nearby lunchers.

Over cocktails Amy handed Rhoda a gift she'd

bought *en route,* a gold bangle in the H-like shape of the Pisces symbol. Rhoda was thrilled with it.

"A thank-you for a lot more than dog-walking," Amy said lightly. "For telling me today would be a whole new day—and has it, ever."

She detailed her morning from the arrival of the mysterious gift, to the visit with Langella and the inquiries at the gallery. "You *told* me so," she concluded, beaming.

When they were having coffee, Rhoda asked quietly, "Is it too soon for you to tell me what happened?"

"No. Not anymore. I just couldn't go through with it." Amy started giving her the blow-by-blow description.

"Incredible." Rhoda's lips were parted in awe and her azure eyes sparkled as she listened to the story. "Cancers are the most unpredictable people," she added in a voice that bubbled with laughter.

As Amy went on with her story, Rhoda could no longer keep from giggling, and even Amy began to see the comical side.

"But what about that man on the plane? He sounds so *nice.*"

"Oh, he was, really." Amy spoke in an absent voice; her thoughts were already on her portfolio.

"What was he *like?*" Rhoda demanded.

"For the life of me, I couldn't 'ID' him if a gun was pointed at my head," Amy protested. But that wasn't entirely true. She'd gotten a fuzzy impression of intense, intelligent gray eyes which projected an aura of toughness and command.

"You must know what he looked like," Rhoda nudged.

"In the state I was in I didn't really care."

Rhoda surveyed her. "Interesting . . . about the collar and leash." She glanced down at Mischief, then at Amy's skirt. "The exact same color of your suit. And that's what you wore on the plane."

It was a bit spooky. Amy tried to picture the tough-handsome man who'd offered help. He'd seemed so concerned. Of course, she'd been around long enough to know what most male "concern" meant. He might be just another married man looking for action.

Funny that the Oz present had made her think of him. He couldn't even know she had a dog, couldn't know her name.

"Anyway," Rhoda said, grinning and lifting her cup, "a big fat *mazel tov.*"

Saluting with her own cup, Amy grinned back. "I'll drink to that."

Today was the first day of the rest of her life, and she wasn't going to look back if she could help it.

CHAPTER TWO

Nick Ransom took absentminded bites of steak Diane and stared blankly at the wall of his favorite restaurant. He couldn't see anything clearly; his mind's eye was on those scenes from last night and this morning. His sequences of detection.

He remembered the expression on the face of his friend at the dog-licensing bureau when Nick asked him to trace a lady from a dog-breed and address. Nick smiled to himself. He remembered Hubert Chandler, his art director's expression. Nick hardly knew art from a jackhammer, and the old mummy had been startled when Nick said he wanted to locate a painter named Amy Hill. Chandler told him she was an up and coming sculptor, associated with Samuel Langella. At that point he raised his elegant white brows. A statue of hers was on view in a nearby park and, of course, at the Langella Gallery there was a display of her work. Nick also learned that she'd worked at the such-and-such museum.

Canceling a meeting and feeling crazy as hell, he went to the Oz Boutique to buy a leash and collar.

From there he'd gone to the park to check out her statue.

It was called "Chores"—a young woman shopper in bronze, which looked incredibly pliant and alive, juggling a small boy, a leashed terrier, and a shopping bag. The bronze woman was laughing, as if life were a circus, not a burden. Even with his untrained eye, he could see that the bronze was technically some piece of work. Nick decided on the spot that he wanted Amy Hill to do the housing-project sculpture—the second time he'd acted on impulse since he was twenty. First she had bowled him over; now her work had. Nick felt the smile on his face.

"What's the joke?" His associate Rod Wales peered at Nick. "Is my approach that bad?"

Nick wasn't *hearing* too well, either. "Give me that last bit again."

Good-naturedly Rod complied. "I like that," he said. "As a matter of fact, I want you to go to Boston for me."

Rod was taken aback. "I thought that was your special baby."

It sure was. He was getting obsessed with buying that Windom land, the very spot his family had been evicted from when he was just a kid. Nick would never get over that resentment. "I think you're just the right baby-sitter," he told Rod. "They really danced me around last week, then begged off for some family thing the last day. Maybe your FFV style can cut it. Beacon Hill has a lot in common with Richmond."

Nick always kidded Rod Wales about his background. He literally belonged to the First Families of Virginia, a fact that someone had leaked to Nick, which embarrassed Rod exceedingly.

"You don't let up, do you?" Rod's retort was amiable. He was not only Nick's right-hand man, he was also his best friend. "Why the sudden switch?"

"The art project, pal." Now Rod looked even more surprised. Nick always left that end of things to him. "Time's a-wasting. I know, I know." He headed Rod off. "You knocked your brains out to find a sculptor and I've been the hold-up. Now I think I've got one."

He'd lucked out, all right. On the woman *and* the sculptor. It was malarkey, of course, claiming that he didn't have time to go to Boston. He didn't *want* to go back to Boston right now.

Enjoying Rod's curious expression, Nick thought, It's true. He'd never let up on anyone or anything. That's what had promoted him from hauling concrete to contracting, level by sweaty, aching level, to the top of the Ransom Tower.

He wasn't going to let up, either, on Project Amy Hill.

Nick excused himself and went to a phone. When he got Chandler, Nick instructed him to set up an interview with her for tomorrow morning.

Carrying her portfolio, Amy entered the futuristic lobby of the famous Ransom Tower, her heart pumping ten miles a minute. Hubert Chandler had *sent* for her. She'd expected to ask for an appointment with him and then wait.

33

She'd spent half the night making some sketches for the project sculpture, the other half awake with stage fright. The very idea of taking on this commission was daunting; it would be the biggest one she'd ever gotten, the most important, bringing her the best kind of exposure.

She glimpsed herself in one of the polished metal panels. Below her dark-brown lacquered straw hat her eyes were huge from excitement and lack of sleep. But she looked all right. Her linen shirtdress was chocolate brown and ivory, striking but understated. She should favorably impress demanding Hubert Chandler. She'd met him once at a crowded function; even briefly he'd lived up to his intimidating reputation.

Rushing past a newsstand Amy glimpsed a headline, paused to look again. A banner shouted: SCULPTOR CASTS BEANTOWN HEIR . . . OFF! Above the headline Jeff Windom's furious face glared from a photo; below it, there was Amy in all her splendor. In her wedding gown at the Logan terminal. She'd been so upset she hadn't even seen someone snap a picture.

A scalding horror splashed over the entire surface of her body. She felt sick, as if she'd been hit in the stomach. Amy had never bought a copy of that rag in her life, but she had to now. She had to read the *Last Word*'s inside story. Giving the vendor exact change, so she wouldn't have to linger— she imagined he gave her an interested glance— Amy took the paper to a quiet corner, turned to the inside feature. There were more pictures: one

34

of herself and Jeff at her opening, the night she'd met him, even one of the Windom mansion.

The revolting report said that the "tight-lipped Windom Brahmins" had had no comment. No one seemed to know why the "swinging mallet-swinger" had reneged, but several "in the know" hinted that Hill had learned at the last minute about a "disappointing marriage settlement."

It was so outrageous, so untrue, that Amy felt like screaming. And there it was, in words and pictures, for the whole world to goggle at. The *Last Word* turned up everywhere, and many people who wouldn't buy it inevitably read its mucky headlines in passing.

Amy folded the offending paper and thrust it into a trash container. She was just going to have to forget it, for now. Somehow. Otherwise the interview would be disastrous; if she let this get to her, she wouldn't project any confidence at all. Anyway, she couldn't picture the Ransom brass reading that awful paper. Especially fastidious Hubert Chandler. Maybe they wouldn't even see it.

Even if they had, she'd be damned if she'd let that libelous report spoil her chances.

She marched into the elevator, straight and proud. A man gave her an admiring glance. With his hand poised at a button, he asked gallantly, "What floor?"

Amy answered evenly, "The top."

That's where she was headed. Nothing was going to stop her.

* * *

"Mr. *Ransom*."

Chandler's tone, when Nick sauntered into the conference room, said what he couldn't: "What are *you* doing here?"

Nick almost laughed out loud. Except for the housing-project art, he'd never taken a direct role in choosing artists. Rod was always Nick's go-between with Chandler. Rod's Ivy League background made it easy for him to deal with Chandler, whereas Nick was more at home on a construction site.

"I'd like to sit in on the interview with Ms. Hill. If it's all right with you," Nick added politely.

Chandler could hardly object. "Why, certainly, Mr. Ransom." But his dismay was evident.

Nick tossed some notes onto the pale circular table. Chandler was sitting with his back to the light. The typical Inquisitor's position, which irritated Nick. He glanced at his watch.

Ten, straight up.

Amy Hill walked through the door, looking a little nervous, but fresh, alert, and absolutely beautiful.

Nick inhaled a quick, excited breath. She was lovelier than he'd remembered.

"Good morning." Her voice was low and sweet as she greeted Chandler.

Then she saw Nick and her cheeks turned pink, then red. She looked trapped.

Damn it, he thought. Besides wanting to see her again, he'd wanted to be the defroster, smooth her

36

way with old Chandler. But now he realized that he should have handled it another way.

It was the man from the plane. First, that newspaper. Now this.

Oh, Lord, he must be Chandler's assistant, she thought. I'll never get the job now. He'd seen her make a fool of herself, watched her blubber on the plane. Maybe he'd even seen the paper downstairs.

"Come in, Ms. Hill," Chandler prompted. She knew she'd been standing there like one of her statues. She tried to pull herself together. "Please sit down," Chandler said.

His painful elegance, his cool, clipped tones were not inviting but they stiffened her backbone. She had to go through with it now.

"Thank you." She was gratified with the calm in her own voice. She smiled at them, set her portfolio on the table and took the chair next to the art director's.

The other man was still standing. He was more attractive than she remembered, now that she had a better look at him—middling tall, with a strong, square-shouldered body, thick black hair; tough-attractive, with a very masculine aura.

"This is Nicholas Ransom, Ms. Hill. Our president," Chandler said. Amy was afraid she was going to pass out.

Nick leaned right across the table and held out his square, strong hand. Very unpresidential body language, was her swift thought. "How do you do. I'm an admirer of yours. I saw 'Chores' and I thought it was just . . . great."

His voice was pleasant and deep, with a rough edge. For an instant she was too surprised to feel nervous. And this time, when she smiled, she could feel the smile was easier. "Thank you very much."

Ransom sat down opposite her, observing her with his light-gray, penetrating eyes. There was nothing in them but kindness and respect. It was as if the incident on the plane had been a nightmare, not real at all. And yet Amy's face hadn't quite cooled off. It *had* happened. And then there was that horrible newspaper downstairs.

She thought, *I really didn't see him that day; I was too upset.* Another flicking glance caught his straight black brows, in sharp contrast to the light, piercing eyes; a mobile mouth with a slight upward curve at one end, a handsome, slightly misshapen nose. A fighter's nose.

Amy sensed Chandler's scrutiny: he seemed to be ticking off her hat, her face and hair, and she hoped she passed inspection. "We received a glowing report on you from Sam Langella." Chandler's warmth was grudging, but it was still warmth.

Ransom leaned forward in his chair, placed his hands flat on the table. The one-sided tilt of his mouth was more emphatic. "All I needed was 'Chores,' Ms. Hill. That was some piece of work."

Amy felt herself relax, leaned back a little in her chair. "It's one of my favorites. As a matter of fact, Mr. Ransom, I visited the site yesterday and got a lot of ideas. I've done some tentative sketches, and they're very much in that style." She indicated her portfolio.

"Let's have a look." Ransom sounded eager; he stood up, came around to her side of the table, keeping a polite distance behind her as she unzipped her portfolio.

But even his comparative nearness made her a bit jumpy. Probably because she was so anxious about this job. So she murmured, "Here, Mr. Ransom. Perhaps you'd like to go through these yourself."

With a quick glance at her, he said, "Thanks." She slid the portfolio to the space in front of the next chair. Still standing, he leaned over and turned the pages. Several times he turned one back, staring at a particular sketch a little longer. "These dogs are so real." Ransom tapped a sketch of a gamboling canine group with one of his big thumbs. "I never even thought of that. Just picturing people, I guess . . ." He gave her a twinkling look. "You understand dogs."

She nodded, smiling.

Ransom turned back to another sketch of a small girl catching a big, light ball with a dancelike motion. Then he gently shut the portfolio. "I'd like you to work for me, Ms. Hill. If you're interested."

Her heart thumped, and warmth spilled over her. "Interested! I'd love to do this project."

Ransom grinned at her. "That's it, then. Let's talk fee."

When he named one it dazzled her, the kind of fee she associated with big names, not a newcomer like herself. "That's . . . that's fine," she gasped. Out of the corner of her eye she got a glimpse of

Hubert Chandler; his elegant white brows had crept up nearly to his hairline.

"Would you get the agreement together, Hubert?" Ransom nodded casually at Chandler. "And . . . may I get a copy of these sketches, Ms. Hill?"

"Of course."

Ransom handed the portfolio to Chandler. Amy glanced after him as he swiftly departed: there was disapproval in the very lines of his well-tailored back, the rhythm of his militant exit.

When she looked back at Ransom, she caught an expression in his keen gray eyes she hadn't seen before. She couldn't read it. His eyes were so light they were like brightly lit windows that obscured the room beyond. She wondered why people thought of dark eyes as the unreadable ones.

She was quick to break the silence. "We'd better talk deadline, Mr. Ransom. It takes a month to cast each piece."

"The middle of October. Let's make it three pieces, under this contract. Exactly what you showed me. Can't go wrong with those. Okay?"

"Okay." She smiled. "I'd like to see the model before I leave, so I can start my miniatures for you."

"Would it be inconvenient for you to come back this evening, about six? To my office?"

It was an odd request. Anyone could show her the model. But she was not going to make any waves with this commission.

"Not at all."

It was little enough concession. Ransom must

have seen the *Last Word* downstairs; now that she'd met him she was convinced those keen gray eyes missed very little. What's more, he'd caught the scene, live, in Boston. But he hired her on the basis of her excellence alone.

And that meant everything.

Sam Langella had always been Amy's informal representative; at Ransom's suggestion she took the agreement to him for approval.

"This is sensational, Amy." Langella looked up at her over the half-glasses that contrasted so oddly with his heavy head and vital physique. "I can't find a wrong comma. Quite a bonus, too . . . Ransom minimizing the specs. Not every patron would be that reasonable, even if it's their fault for doing things at the last minute."

"Chandler gave me the impression I'm being overpaid," Amy said dryly.

"Bull. You deserve every penny," Langella assured her. He chuckled. "Makes me feel good. Everybody likes to be right."

She smiled at his smug expression.

"I'm awfully glad for you," he added.

"Not half as glad as I am, maestro. You know, if it weren't for you, I wouldn't be signing these agreements." She knew gratitude embarrassed Langella, but she had to say it anyway.

He scowled to hide his pleasure. "Hell, I didn't give you your talent."

Langella had, in a way, but she didn't pursue it. She put the agreements in her bag and got up. "Thanks again, Sam, for looking at these. I'd better not keep you." As usual he was in the midst of another urgent enterprise. But she couldn't leave until she found out if he'd seen that rotten story.

"Sam—"

"Look, Amy—"

Both names came out at once. Langella smiled a bit tightly. "After you."

She blurted, "I was going to ask you if you'd seen the *Last Word* today."

Langella looked relieved. "You saved me a lot of bother. I was going to try to find out, without asking, if *you* had. No, I didn't see it myself, but Marta did. In the supermarket. She called me, gave me all the gory details. You're not going to let that garbage get you down?"

She sat down again on the edge of the chair. "Damn it, Sam. It can't help me. Even if people in the art world aren't exactly subscribers," her sarcasm was heavy, "it's got to leak out. The name 'Hill' will be some kind of . . . joke. That kind of limelight might be good for a crazy pop artist. Not a traditionalist like me."

"Maybe," Langella admitted. "But come *on,* Amy. Every great artist in history has had some kind of scandal attached to him. Van Gogh cut off his *ear,* for God's sake. This thing'll die down. You haven't committed a crime. They won't be looking for a body." He was trying hard to tease her out of her doldrums. "Lighten up. It didn't stop Ransom, did it? Nobody with any brains will pay any attention. I mean it. In another week, the whole thing'll blow right over. They'll be zeroing in on some other so-called Beautiful People."

She rose. Langella was probably right; he nearly always was.

"You've made your point." She managed to smile at him.

"Damn right I have. Don't let this interfere with your project. Personally, I'd love to knock those reporters' heads together for you . . ." He grinned wickedly. "But it'd just make some more headlines."

She loved him for that. He'd made her feel a hundred times better; so much so that she called Rhoda with the news and made a date for lunch.

When Rhoda arrived at the restaurant, Amy could tell from her face that she'd seen the paper, too. Her expression was an uneasy blend of nervousness and pleasure.

"Don't tell me," Amy announced. "You saw the *Last Word*."

Rhoda sat down and her whole body relaxed. It was so much like the encounter with Langella that Amy had to laugh.

"You were going to feel around and find out if *I'd* seen it. Right?"

Rhoda stared. "Have you taken up witching?"

Amy told her about Langella.

"*That* thing," Rhoda dismissed the offending newspaper with a shrug. "Langella's absolutely right. Now, tell me about *everything*."

She interjected a hundred excited questions into Amy's report. "What did I tell you?" she demanded.

They had hardly been served when she prodded,

"What about Ransom? Are his ears set close to his head? What are his hands like? Is he married?"

"If I didn't love you, I wouldn't be able to stand you," Amy retorted. "A, I didn't look at his ears. B, his hands are big and square . . . I *think* . . . and C, I don't *care* whether he's married or not."

"I knew it, I knew it!" Rhoda was undiscouraged. "He must be a Capricorn—that's dynamite for your Cancer!"

Amy smiled good-naturedly. "Ask me about the *commission,* Rhoda."

"Okay. Now that we've cleared up Mr. Capricorn, tell me about the commission."

Amy did in great detail. When she mentioned the fee, Rhoda's blue eyes widened.

"Oh, Amy, I'm so *happy.* You deserve every bit of it." She looked thoughtful. "You know, Ransom must be a very special kind of man. Too smart to be influenced by all that . . . nonsense." She smiled her impish smile. "I still think there's more to it than your expertise."

"Well, thanks a lot. In other words, as a sculptor I'm a great sex symbol."

"You know I didn't mean it that way. But you don't realize how beautiful you are. As a matter of fact, that's one of the nicest things about you."

Amy was still a bit annoyed, though, at the implication. Her expression must have said it, because Rhoda looked remorseful.

"I'm sorry."

"Forget it." Amy reached over and patted her hand. To get the spotlight off herself, she said, "You know, for somebody so obsessed with romance, you don't practice what you preach. I don't think you've had four dates in the last five years."

"That's different," Rhoda insisted. "I've *had* my romance. Since Jake died there just hasn't been anyone who could . . . come up to him. I'm past it, kiddo."

"*Past* it." Amy studied Rhoda's flawless skin, her bright blue eyes, her drift of brief blond hair. "Just look in the mirror."

Rhoda was flustered, with the tables turned. She countered, "It's you we're talking about. I think a six o'clock appointment sounds . . . interesting. But I'll stop picking on you. The main thing is, you're being recognized the way you should be. And it can only get better."

Amy tried to hang on to that for the rest of the afternoon. She'd never had Rhoda's carefree optimism. And she knew her friend had shrugged off that story in an attempt to convince Amy that it meant nothing.

She thought gloomily, *The agreements aren't signed yet.*

Before she left that evening, Amy changed into a simple black silk dress to wear to Ransom Tower. Sightly, not sexy, she decided, when she stepped into the shining lobby, and checked herself out in the polished metal walls. Just the way she wanted to look. Her leather-trimmed wicker briefcase was a nice businesslike touch.

The newsstand was still open; she couldn't help noticing that the supply of *Last Word*s was gone. Amy flashed back to the morning and how she'd felt when she first saw that headline—prickly and chagrined. She was beginning to feel that way again.

On top of that she recalled Rhoda's hints about a "romantic dinner." Amy felt a twinge: she'd been so sure this morning that she'd been commissioned for her work, and not romance.

Ransom could be one of those married men who kept an office hideaway. It was such a dismal idea she refused to consider it.

When the elevator softly deposited her on the penthouse floor, she saw a chic, gray-haired woman waiting in the reception area. She approached Amy, smiling. Her perfect black shirtwaist dress, her cloud of silvery hair, were the height of elegance, yet Amy sensed a maternal quality in her.

"I'm Esther Faber, Mr. Ransom's secretary. He and Mr. Wales should be here soon. I'll show you to the office."

He and Mr. Wales. So much for her seduction fantasy. She followed Esther Faber into an immense corner office. In contrast to the reception area it had a pleasant air of tradition.

"Would you like a cold drink?" the secretary asked her.

"I'd love one, thanks." Esther Faber came back with Amy's choice, then left her alone in a comfortable conference area. She looked out over the fabulous evening view of Chicago, abashed at misreading Ransom. He obviously didn't go for glamorous secretaries; he was bringing an associate to their meeting. Her spirits rose. It had been idiotic to write such a corny script.

She couldn't wait to start the miniatures. As soon as she got home tonight, she'd go to work.

"Good evening."

Ransom was coming toward her, giving her a friendly smile. With him was a tall, amiable red-haired man with something vaguely familiar about him.

And, to her pleased surprise, two beautiful Dobermans. "Well, *hello*." Reacting to her tone, the dogs approached her, and she petted them. They were deep black with unique markings; one had a russet ring around one eye, the other had two rings, like spectacles.

She looked up at Ransom; he was smiling from ear to ear. He recalled himself. "Ms. Hill, my associate. Rod Wales."

Amy extended her hand. She liked Wales's looks; he had neat features and sharp black eyes. There was something, still, faintly familiar about him and she reacted to him warmly. "I saw the sketches," Wales said. "They're marvelous." His soft consonants and melodic vowels sounded "high Southern," as Rhoda would put it. Something like Bostonian.

The idea disturbed her; she wondered if it had shown in her face, because she caught an odd glint in Ransom's eyes. To hide her expression, she leaned over again to pet one of the Dobermans.

"And last, but not least," Ransom said, "Ace . . . and Deuce."

He walked to a phone and spoke into it, asking

Esther Faber for iced coffee. Amy liked his easy manner with her and with Wales. He certainly wasn't a snappish, high-powered tycoon.

He sat down in the chair next to hers. "So, was the agreement satisfactory?"

"Yes, of course." She handed him the copies she'd signed. He scribbled his black, jagged signature on them rapidly, with impatience. "You have carte blanche, whatever you need," he said to Amy. He named some perks.

"I'm impressed." She was. "I had no idea I'd get such royal treatment."

"You call the shots." Ransom looked at his watch. "Would you join us for dinner? I asked you here at a bad time and we're having something brought in from the Cambria."

He made it sound like fast food. To Amy the Cambria was glowing memories of silky mousses, delicate entrées.

"Well, yes. I'd like to."

They made their way into a small, cozy dining room beyond the office. The dogs trotted after. "Hope you don't mind the beasts," Ransom said lightly.

"Not at *all.* I have a dog, too. A Scottie. I'd never dream of shutting him out."

As they sat down at the table, Amy thought she saw a quick glance between the two men. "How pretty," she murmured.

The round table was set with exquisite china, crystal, and massive silver; there were lighted candles in heavy crystal holders, a centerpiece of anemones.

"Our home away from home," Wales drawled. "Nick and I spend a lot of time here."

"Unlucky bachelors," Ransom commented.

So he wasn't married. That would answer one of Rhoda's questions. But the rest of it was amusing: Amy was having a very glamorous dinner . . . with his associate and two dogs in the bargain.

A waiter in a dinner jacket was setting a trio of hors d'oeuvres before them—scallops arranged on a bed of spinach pasta around a center of red caviar.

Rod Wales forked his scallops and teased, "I hope we won't get the usual lecture on 'Bahstan' seafood."

The very mention of Boston was both painful and embarrassing to Amy. Ransom caught her eye.

"You won't," he said casually. "This is very good. You must have been sculpting for a long time, Ms. Hill."

"Yes. Since I was about fourteen." She was grateful to him for changing the subject. Obviously Wales didn't know about her. Ransom hadn't told him and they were evidently close friends. She liked that; it made them conspirators of a sort. She found herself warming to him, telling them both about her early interest in art.

Soon she and Wales were engrossed in an enthusiastic exchange about sculpture. Ransom mostly listened. And then she knew who Wales reminded her of.

Jeff.

Wales was nowhere near as good-looking but he

had the same polished, aristocratic manner, the same Ivy League style.

After they'd had their coffee, he asked her if she wanted to check out the model. He opened another door and gestured her into the living room of an apartment beyond. The housing project model was on a splendid oak side table. Ransom indicated a drawer in it. "I think you'll find everything you need."

She thanked him absently and stood back, squinting at the model, forgetting everything except the delicious problem of which piece belonged where. She could already see the completed sculpture—one in the oval park there, another on the grass beside the stairs; the third dramatizing the building complex entrance.

Opening the drawer in the table she found a pad, a beautiful walnut-and-brass pen and matching ruler, other implements. Soon she was measuring, considering, taking notes, as if she were completely alone.

She was dimly aware that Wales was sprawled on a couch, scratching the Dobies' ears and that Nicholas Ransom stood a little way off.

Finished, she came to. She glanced at Ransom, smiling. His sharp gray eyes gleamed; he was smiling back at her.

"You really took off. You reminded me of me." His penetrating eyes sparkled with warmth. It was the first time he'd revealed himself and the atmosphere was faintly charged.

She was conscious of a pleasing scent from his skin and clothes, a mysterious blend of fresh air and woodsmoke and pine. He positively exuded masculinity in his solid, easy stance, the heavy biceps straining the sleeves of his jacket, the slope of his massive shoulders. The back of Amy's neck had a prickly sensation, just at the roots of her hair, her body unreasonably cold, then warm. It was very unsettling.

She said in a rush, "If I can just show you what I have in mind . . ."

Ransom stepped forward at once, to bend over the model; she could feel his glance on her hands as she gestured. "Perfect. You've got it. Come here, Rod."

Wales strolled over. "I like it, Nick."

"I think I'll say good night, then. I can't wait to get started."

Ransom grinned. "Now you're one of us. Slaves, Incorporated. Look, let me drive you home," he suggested.

She said something about getting a cab but he was insistent. "The guys want a ride, anyway," he said casually. Amy had to laugh when the dogs' ears came to attention. It was clearly a word they knew and loved.

"When you put it that way, how can I refuse?"

But when they walked back through the reception area then descended in the private elevator, she was silent. Being alone with Nick Ransom, after their introduction to each other in Boston, was more unnerving than anything else that had happened all day.

CHAPTER THREE

In the private elevator, Amy sensed tension in Ransom as well. The air between them was weighted with unspoken words, the unmentionable subject of their Boston encounter. A topic, she thought wryly, that would have to be as carefully avoided as some blatant defect of feature.

She felt a nervous giggle threaten to explode then let out a breath of relief when they reached the basement garage.

The Dobies made a beeline for a sleek Mercedes. As soon as Ransom opened the door, they jumped into the front seat.

"Not tonight, guys."

Ransom's deep, rough voice was gentle, with a humorous intonation. Amy had an immediate reaction to the voice: it affected her as strongly as his proximity had a little while before. Her nervousness was heightened.

The dogs immediately got out and jumped into the back.

"I never saw dogs so perfectly trained." Amy was surprised at how calmly that came out, glad to break the silence.

Ransom was gratified. "The reward system. Never punishment . . . just withholding the reward."

She got in the car, remembering Jeff's indifference to Mischief. Something very near affection mingled with her other feelings about Nick Ransom. He seemed to have invested a lot of emotion in his pets, just as she had, and she wondered if he might be a lonely man.

Yet the very sense of rapport with him made her feel wary. If there was one thing she was determined to avoid, it was getting close to another man for a long time to come.

She fell into silence again as they drove away, noticing he hadn't asked for directions. But he probably knew her address from the agreement, as a builder knew every inch of Chicago.

Ace and Deuce braced themselves against the front seat, leaning on their paws. Ransom said quietly, "Take it easy, fellows."

She was amazed at how quickly the dogs backed off, obeying, and said quickly, "That's all right. Actually, I rather liked it."

"Hear that?" Ransom said to the dogs. "The lady's inviting you. Come."

They resumed their position against the seat and one of them nuzzled Amy's hair. She thought, *It's impossible to be cool and withdrawn in a situation like this,* and she found herself relaxing, some of her uneasiness dispelled.

By the time they got to the loft, she was feeling quite warm toward Nick Ransom.

She turned and smiled at him. "Thank you, Mr. Ransom."

There was a bright gleam in his fierce gray eyes. He looked as if he wanted to say something but thought better of it.

"Don't mention it."

"I'll be in touch soon, with the miniatures," she promised, with a sudden desire to remind him—and herself—of business.

"Wonderful." His eyes still had that brilliant gleam. As she got out, he added, "I'll wait and see you in. Good night, Ms. Hill."

"Good night. And you, too." She patted the Dobies.

When she was walking to the door she heard Nick Ransom whistle; turning, saw the dogs jump over to the front seat.

Mischief sniffed at her clothes as she opened the loft door, excited by the scent of other dogs, and let out an interested bark. She took him out for a brief run and hurried back, eager to get to work again.

She was picturing the first tiny clay model she would attack—the group of playful dogs that would go in the center of the model's green-painted oval representing grass.

Stripping for action, she got into her loose, clay-stained jumpsuit and went into the studio. Mischief trotted after. The intelligent Scottie never touched her work but he always watched, fascinated, when Amy sketched or modeled. Now he took his place beside her on the floor next to the modeling table.

Perversely, now that she was free to start, Amy was abruptly distracted by the events of the incredible day . . . wonderful, terrible, and confusing.

The confusing part had to do with her strange, mixed feelings for Nick Ransom. He was a fascinating, complex man, so complex that she *couldn't* react simply to him, she decided.

He clearly was a high-powered, independent company president. So independent he'd commissioned her with a total disregard of the apparent craziness he'd first witnessed in her.

On the other hand, there was a gentleness about him, evidenced in his strong attachment to his dogs. And a mystery, too. She wondered if he'd ever been married; it was unusual for someone his age still to be a bachelor. The style of his penthouse apartment including the china and silver, had been heavy and masculine, hinting at all-male dinners in the past. There were not many signs of a woman's touch.

Worst of all, Amy thought, in an already complicated situation, another dimension had been added—her brief, sharp physical reactions to him at various moments tonight.

The last thing on earth she needed was reacting like that to another man. In fact, it amazed her that she *could* react so soon after Jeff. She'd always been something of a museum piece in that area, too fastidious for casual sex, pouring all her emotion into her art.

From the time she was ten years old she'd haunted Chicago museums. There she glimpsed the beauty and splendor denied to her at home.

Her father was a despondent failure who drank too much. And even then, Amy could see what marriage did to her mother, who looked a decade older than she was. It had been difficult financially after Amy's father died and she'd worked illegally, lying about her age. Her high school art classes had been the high point of her life.

She decided then she wanted to be a sculptor. Sculpture was solid, as her life had never been. She plunged into her work, scraped up money for art instruction but mostly was self-taught. Langella had been her mainstay, urging her on, sharing his studio with her when she needed to do pieces too big for the apartment she shared with her mother.

Yes, her work had been her life, kept her going through everything. And she mustn't forget that now.

Snapping out of her mood, Amy referred to her sketch of the dog-group and decided to make a change. Instead of the dogs she'd shown Wales and Ransom, she started forming a group of four. One was a Scottie, very like Mischief, one a happy-looking mutt and two were sleek and gentle Dobermans.

With nimble fingers and delicate tools, Amy began to bring the tiny bodies to life, working faster, more easily than she ever had before; so inspired she didn't even need an attitude sketch to guide her.

Finally she sat back, astonished at how quickly the rough miniatures had gone. The details still had to be added, but the stances of the bodies were already beautiful, with joy and grace in every line.

The dogs looked like they were dancing. The mixed breed, she thought, was a marvelous touch —a plain, good dog for good plain people, the kind who'd live in the housing project.

Now for the detail work. She smiled to herself and petted Mischief. "You'd better get comfortable. This is going to be a long night."

As if he'd understood, the Scottie lay down again, contemplating her with bright but sleepy eyes.

Later, when Amy was finished, she turned the small stand: the miniature was good. Very good, from every angle. And she realized that some shadowy feeling she'd never had before had gone into the figures.

An emotion she only half-comprehended.

When Nick Ransom returned to his penthouse office after dropping Amy off, Rod was there with all the Boston stuff already spread out on the desk.

"Great," Nick said. "Let's get started. It's been a day and a half." The dogs sprawled by his chair as he sat down.

"It's been a good one. It's a load off my mind to have the sculpture wrapped up. I thought we'd never find one."

Nick didn't answer. Rod eyed him, and went on, "I can see why you didn't like the others' work. I think this one's terrific. She's got a real human touch. How'd you run across her?"

"Through the friend of a friend." Nick knew Rod was curious; he wasn't usually this cagey about things with Rod Wales. *"Okay,"* he prodded.

"Let's do it. Where's your game plan again?" Nick glanced over the papers. "Here we go." He began to read the memorandum with closer attention than he'd given it earlier.

Rod was still studying Nick with interest, not the memorandum. *He really was curious about Amy Hill,* Nick thought, *but he sure as hell wasn't going to get anything out of him.* Without thinking, Nick said, "Reach in that middle cabinet, would you? That Washington letter is right there on the top."

Then he recalled, too late, that it wasn't on top. Something else was, though. "What the hell is *this,* Nick?"

Puzzled, Rod pulled out a copy of the *Last Word.* He saw the other forty-nine copies under the first one.

Nick swore softly.

Rod, squatting before the cabinet, turned to look at him. "Good Lord, there must be a hundred of these things here."

"Fifty," Nick corrected.

Rod found the letter in the cabinet and got up. "What gives?"

Nick waited.

Rod glanced at the paper again, whistled, and opened it out. "Amy *Hill?*" He skimmed the photos and the headline and turned to the inside page, giving it a lightning read. "I can't believe it." Rod shook his red head. "She seemed so *together* . . . so bright."

"She is."

Rod looked at Nick. "You know, this isn't the greatest recommendation, buddy."

Nick felt his pressure shoot up. "You're smarter than that, Wales. You know what these damned papers are like. They wouldn't know the truth if it bit them. That's a dumb reaction. Exactly why I bought these things. I didn't want it spread all over the building." He glared at Rod.

"Wait a minute," Rod protested. "I know these papers are ridiculous. They distort everything. But they can't distort *that* much. The fact remains, the woman ran right out of the church. That doesn't indicate a very . . . steady temperament," he concluded mildly.

"It indicates guts. And brains," Nick countered. "She had the sense to dump that pretty boy. How many women would have the nerve to do what she did?"

"Not many." Rod didn't sound very convinced. "Not many would reject this guy, either." He flipped back to Jeff Windom's picture. "Rich as hell and he looks like a damned movie star."

Rod noticed that Nick had an instant, jealous reaction when he referred to Windom's good looks. Rod continued. "It just occurred to me. *Windom*. This is like a 1930s movie: you're after the Windom land, and the girl who got away is working for us."

He studied Nick and it suddenly occurred to him why Nick had bought the fifty copies.

"I'm sticking my neck out, pal. But I have a feeling you're interested in more than the sculpture."

He's got me there, Nick thought. He was sweating under his collar.

"Hey, Nick. I'm sorry." Embarrassed, Rod gathered up the Boston papers, stowing them into his briefcase. "It's none of my business. Only the sculpture is," he amended, smiling. "And I think that's going to be great. She's a lovely woman. Like perfume compared to vinegar, in comparison to—" he broke off.

"Janet. Why not say it? It's true."

"I've got foot-in-the-mouth disease tonight. So I may as well go on being offensive, Nick. It'll be a tough assignment."

"What the hell does that mean?" Nick demanded, getting hot all over again. "You wouldn't be interested yourself, by any chance?" Nick hadn't forgotten how comfortable Amy had been with Rod. Maybe, because of his background, he reminded her of Pretty-Face Windom.

"Not by any chance. You know I only date blondes. Simmer down. I meant she's gone through a big upheaval, maybe the biggest one in her life. I'd bet on that, because she doesn't seem like the flighty type, not when you talk to her awhile. It might be a cold day in hell before she teams up again."

"So what are you, 'Dear Abby'?" Nick stood up, a little ashamed of his irrational jealousy of Rod. "I can wait. Now get out of here. I'm tired." He smiled to neutralize his sharp order.

"You're the boss. See you guys."

Rod gave Nick a salute and walked out.

Nick strode through the dining room, shining

and empty now, flashing back to their dinner. He liked everything about that woman, from her big, expressive eyes and lovely face to her soft, slender body. After a whole evening with her, when they'd been, at times, so near each other, the mental picture made him sweat.

He jerked off his loosened tie on his way to the bedroom, snatching off his shirt as he walked. Nick abandoned the rest of his clothes, strewing them helter-skelter en route to the shower.

What he needed, he thought sardonically, was a very cold one. He stood in the frigid, needled spray, gasping and thinking about her.

She was more appealing every time he saw her. There was something so different about her—she had a quiet, almost old-fashioned sweetness. Yet she was ambitious, courageous, and stubborn.

Toweling himself harshly, Nick grinned as he remembered the proud way she'd entered old Chandler's sanctum; her poise at dinner; her eagerness to get to work. Amy Hill's life meant something to her. She meant something to herself.

Amy Hill was gifted and independent, everything Janet was not. Even with the dogs.

It was like she and Nick Ransom were made for each other.

Wandering back into his bedroom, Nick examined that cornball expression. He'd never figured, in a million years, that he could feel like this about a woman he'd known less than a week.

But he did. And that was that. He put on some pajama pants, feeling antsy enough to punch a hole in the wall. What Rod had said was true: it was going to be a tough assignment. She'd just gotten out of one entanglement and she wasn't ready for another.

Besides, what did he really have to offer her, in comparison to that Boston golden boy? Even if the guy had been a certified jerk—and he had to be, to let Amy get away—his looks alone were a hard act to follow. Looks, education, a family tree with its roots in the Year One.

Nick lit a cigarette and paced the carpet. The way she'd warmed up right away to Rod still bothered him. If she liked Windom's type, and Rod's, then a Nick Ransom wouldn't even be in the ballpark.

If this Jeff was like old man Windom, he was about as contemporary as George the Third, and about as democratic.

Nick swore, thinking of the dead-end land negotiations in Boston. He sprawled out on the bed. Well, now he knew what the "family affair" was that canceled his last meeting. Dealing with the Windoms was an uphill run. But he wasn't through, not by a long shot.

He was going to get that Windom land. The housing project would not only benefit a lot of working people, but it would be a great payback to the very ones who'd evicted his own people such a long time ago.

Nick squashed his cigarette, turned off the light and stared out at the glittering skyline of Chicago.

Now the Windoms had two things he wanted: the land, and the kind of commitment Amy Hill had once made to their son and heir.

She was going to need a lot of patience, just like the land deal.

That was something Nick Ransom had in abundance; it would be a long time before it was used up.

At least he had a foot in the door. Now she was working for him. He was going to take every sweet advantage that he could.

CHAPTER FOUR

When the phone rang on Saturday afternoon, Amy's first response was dread. She hoped it wouldn't be a reporter. It couldn't be business.

"Ms. Hill?"

She didn't recognize the man's voice.

"Nick Ransom."

So it *was* business. Relieved, she answered with level politeness.

"It's a bad time to call," he apologized. "And I know the models will be delivered Monday. The thing is, I've got to go away this weekend, and I'm very anxious to see them. Would you let me drop over, about five? I'd be very grateful."

The only answer she could make was "Of course."

Amy hung up half-irritated, half-puzzled. His thank-you had been so fervent that her irritation shamed her a little, but the puzzlement remained. She'd never met anyone in Ransom's position with such an avid interest in one project, a project that must be a fraction of his enormous enterprises.

But she was glad, too, in a way. His visit would push her into a proper tidying up—of the loft and herself—which she'd let slide for the last several days. When she was on a "roll" at work, it was around the clock, with long, forgetful hours, and only Mischief got the necessary attention.

Besides, it would take her mind off the fact that this was her first full weekend alone.

She was glad now she hadn't packed the models yet; she'd planned that for tomorrow morning before her afternoon movie date with Rhoda.

It was already three thirty and there was plenty left to do because she'd slept so late. She got to it, and since the weather was warm and muggy she made iced coffee and got into a peach-colored sundress and bare sandals.

Her small antique clock in the living room was chiming five when the bell rang.

When she opened her door she greeted Nick Ransom with a sense of surprise: he looked so much younger, so different in his casual clothes. His pale gray shirt emphasized the dramatic blackness of his hair, pointed up the light silvery gray of his piercing eyes. She hadn't seen his arms before: they were very muscular and deeply tanned. His masculinity was apparent, making her feel oddly nervous.

Mischief, as usual, was right at her heels. When Ransom spoke Amy saw the little dog's tail start to wag.

"You're very nice to let me come," Ransom said, smiling as he walked in. "Well! This must be Mischief."

Now that was strange, she thought. She didn't

remember having mentioned her dog's name. But she must have.

Nick squatted down and gently petted Mischief, whose response was immediate and fervent. The sight warmed Amy to Nick all over again.

"Can I give you some iced coffee? It's warm outside."

Ransom's pale eyes brightened, but he said apologetically, "I don't want to . . . hold you up."

"Not at all."

When she brought the coffee, his keen glance flickered over her face, dress and hair before wandering around the living-room space. "This is sensational. You designed it yourself." That was a statement, not a question, full of wistful envy. A strange reaction for a man with his resources.

"Yes. I did." She *was* proud of her imaginative partitioning, the "still-lifes" she'd created with cushions and colors, accessories and other arrangements.

Ransom put down his glass and stood abruptly. "You're being so nice and patient. I'm taking up your time. Lead me to the miniatures and I'll get out of your hair." His smile was so charming that when she protested it wasn't just polite.

Nevertheless she showed him into the studio, as Mischief capered ahead. Once again Ransom looked around with eager interest. "You've done a great job here also." He grinned, tested the floor with his foot. "Sound floors. What was here, heavy machinery?" She nodded.

He went to the table, leaned to examine the miniatures.

66

Amy reviewed the pieces from a new perspective: the quartet of dogs, the girl with a ball, a pair of young married lovers sitting on a bench, enclosed in their own magic. She realized she'd brought her most profound longings and beliefs into their execution. There was a statement there she hadn't made since "Chores." Even in that work there hadn't been quite this feeling.

"They're so alive," Ransom murmured. "Full size, they'll be . . . overpowering."

She was elated by his praise.

"You know," he said, looking up at her from his position of scrutiny, "I don't know zip about these things." He straightened. "But one thing for sure, you've got something here that . . . talks to *people*. The kind I come from."

So that was it, she decided. She should have known. She and Ransom had started life in much the same way, it seemed. "You don't know how that pleases me. It means I've achieved what I've always strived for—to make something utterly beautiful, yet realistic. Art that steps down off the pedestal and touches people. I'm from 'plain people,' too."

"I'd never think of you as plain," he quipped. His keen eyes admired her. Her skin felt abruptly warm and she made a restless movement, stepping back. He seemed to pick up on her withdrawal.

"I've done it again," he said.

"Done what?"

"Barged in around dinnertime. May I make up for it by offering you some?"

She hesitated. For a man who ran a multimillion-dollar operation his apparent naïveté was a bit much. Once maybe, yes. Twice was a ploy.

"Could I?"

Why on earth not? she decided. Maybe this was more than business to him, and suddenly she didn't mind at all. She was rather glad.

"Yes, I'd like that."

He looked so pleased she was touched. "How would you like to go out to my summer place? It'll be pleasant now, and we can bring your dog, too."

"That sounds wonderful." She went to get a bag and came back to leash Mischief. Ransom watched while she fastened the elegant pink harness from the Oz.

When Amy straightened she surprised an odd expression on Ransom's face; he was studying her with a one-sided smile and his sharp eyes twinkled. "Pretty," he murmured. She was struck with a wild idea: Ransom had sent the gift. But how could he have known about Mischief then?

They took the Outer Drive, passing a series of yacht harbors, the Gold Coast of luxury condos and apartments. Ransom said casually, "I'm not the country type, really. I was born in a city, lived in cities all my life. Too much ozone chokes me."

She laughed. "Me, too. I can't breathe in pure air. But it sounds good today."

Amy remembered how Jeff had sneered at Chicago, which was still the Wild West to his stuffy clan. Ransom obviously liked the city as much as she did and that gave them another thing in common.

In a little while they were leaving the Drive, heading into a thickly wooded area.

Ransom pulled into a road that led to a big brown-shingled house, big enough for a family of four.

Braking, he glanced at her with his tilted smile, as if he'd read her mind. "I have a thing about space. I grew up in a crowded situation."

"You're talking to a *sculptor,*" she countered. "I nearly sculpted my mother out of our apartment. This is marvelous."

"Glad you like it." Ransom opened her door and she got out, unleashing Mischief. From somewhere behind the house, she heard the Dobies' deep bark, then saw them galloping around the side of the house to greet Ransom.

They sniffed at Mischief and he sniffed back. Ransom chuckled. "He's not intimidated."

"He never is."

Amy heard a whistle. The Dobies took off.

"Dinnertime. How about Mischief?"

"He's had his, thank you." They went into the house, and Ransom called out, "Kim?"

A slim young Korean man came in from the rear. He had a nice smile, she thought.

"This is Ms. Hill, Kim. And Mischief. Can you find some human food for us?"

"Sure thing. I'll put on another wienie." Kim nodded amiably and disappeared.

"Make yourself at home," Ransom invited.

She glanced around the rather austere living room. The place was obviously a man's room, like the penthouse apartment. Only one painting was hung over the empty fireplace, a harbor scene.

Amy's glance passed over the oil, taking in the heavy striped curtains, massive, earth-colored furniture and sparse ornaments. But there was a superb set of hi-fi components and other electronic gadgets, and there was an air of comfort about the place.

She said so, sitting down on the big, heavy couch covered in brown corduroy.

"It was bare as your hand until Kim took over," Ransom said. As if summoned, the young Korean came in smiling; he was carrying an earthenware vase full of orange and yellow wildflowers.

"See what I mean?" Ransom chuckled. Mischief came trotting in and jumped up on the couch beside Amy. She noticed a dining area in the corner of the room; Kim set the vase of wildflowers in the center of a round oak table, taking mats from a sideboard.

When he went out, Ransom busied himself at the bar.

"I like him," Amy said simply.

Ransom beamed. "He's the best. Can I fix you something?"

She asked for a sherry and he brought it to her, with a small whiskey for himself. He sprawled in a big chair opposite her, sipped and continued, "Kim's a refugee. He's a student at the university. Also a very good painter—they tell me"—he mocked his own comparative ignorance and that touched her—"and the only reason I'm lucky enough to have him is because he likes hiding out here in the summer."

Ransom grinned. She thought about his unusual relationship with his employees. So Kim was not an ordinary servant, just as Esther Faber and Rod Wales were not ordinary employees, either. She liked that, very much. There was something so . . . very likable about this man; he'd upset all her preconceived notions of high-powered, cold-blooded tycoons. And she felt something else in him—an odd wistfulness, a loneliness, almost a hunger for some unattained goal.

But that was a bit much; she was writing quite a fantasy script. He was the man who had everything, really. Money, power, success.

She realized she'd been awkwardly silent. To have something to say, she remarked on the painting over the fireplace. "That's a magnificent oil." Looking at it more closely, she saw what it depicted. Before she thought, she blurted, "Why, it's Boston Harbor."

Ransom's glass was arrested halfway to his lips. Noticing her embarrassed expression, he sipped and set down his glass. "Yes." His tone was casual, light. "That's where I come from, actually."

She looked up, meeting his level gaze.

It was time they stopped dancing around the subject, she decided. This was ridiculous. He'd been walking on eggs about the subject of Boston ever since he'd hired her.

"Which reminds me," she said steadily, keeping her look on his, "I want to thank you for . . . the way you've handled Boston, Mr. Ransom."

He let out his breath, as if a burden had been lifted and his smile was wide and warm. "Nothing to thank me for," he murmured. "I want to *congratulate* you. For the way you've been 'handling Boston.'"

She flushed, embarrassed but grateful at the same time. "I must admit," she said with a new sense of openness and release, "my blood froze when you turned up at that interview."

"I know." His face was very serious now. "I should have prepared you for that. But I was so eager to see you, uh your work," he amended, "that I just invited myself."

It sounded as if he'd been about to say, "see *you.*" But she hurried on, "You've never been anything but extremely tactful, Mr. Ransom. I appreciate it."

He started to say something else, but she heard Kim coming back with dishes. They were silent while he set the table. Then, when he'd gone out again, Ransom said quietly, "I hope you won't be offended if I ask you something."

She waited, not knowing at all what to expect, hesitating to commit herself.

He grinned at her hesitation. "Nothing monumental. Except, well, just dispensing with this 'Ms.' and 'Mister' stuff. I'm much more comfortable with 'Nick.'"

She smiled back. "And I with 'Amy.'"

His eyes lit up at the small concession. After all, she reflected, it was silly for them to keep on using formal titles, after what had happened in Boston. It was almost an intimate connection.

Amy felt new warmth under her skin, and Ransom misunderstood her chagrin. He quickly changed the subject, and once again she was moved by his sensitive awareness of her discomfort. "I hope you like trout. Not sushi but grilled," he said. "Kim does a great job with it."

"It's my favorite."

"Good. Another?" Ransom held up his glass. She shook her head, feeling unusually calm and relaxed. It was amazing how much at home she felt; she'd hardly noticed Kim's goings and comings.

The Dobies trotted in, winded, and plumped down on the big rag rug between Amy and Nick. Mischief was asleep, snoring.

Nick opened a wooden box and offered her a cigarette. Lighting their two, he leaned back in his chair. "I liked that mutt in the dog piece. That's really my kind of dog. I got the Dobies by accident. They were in a—hell of a situation, and I took them out of it. But where I grew up, a Doberman was something you saw in World War Two movies." He chuckled.

"It was the same for me. I found Mischief in a shelter."

It was time for dinner. Kim served them gracefully and disappeared.

Amy commented on the candles and flowers. "Kim's a treasure."

"I don't usually get this kind of service. It's the first time we've had a lady here."

There was no easy reply to that, so she didn't make one. If that was true she must be special. She continued to be surprised at Nick's frankness—the style of a much younger, less worldly man—coupled with his reticence. He certainly didn't have a "way with women." That made her feel very secure. Jeff had always been so damned *smooth,* as if he'd practiced the things he said to her on a lot of other women.

Sipping the pale gold wine, sampling the subtly flavored speckled trout, she remarked, "Kim has a sense of humor. *This* is the 'extra wienie'?"

"That's another reason I like to have him around."

His glance met Amy's over the candlelight.

She took a sip of her wine, pleading with him in silence, *Don't do this to me.* She felt so good, so relaxed with him. If there was any way for them to be friends, she wanted to find it, but there was something in his manner that suggested he wanted more. And in spite of all that happened to her Amy couldn't help being aware of his strong magnetism, his attractiveness as a man. She wasn't ready for that. She wasn't sure she would ever be again.

"So now you'll be starting the hard part," he remarked abruptly. "With the work."

His ability to read her was astonishing, Amy thought. Every time he picked up on her unease, he had a marvelous way of switching the subject. She supposed that was one of the gifts that had gotten him where he was in the business world.

"Oh, yes. You see things very differently from the standpoint of six feet . . . when you've been working with inches."

"I can imagine," he said companionably. "For me it's always been feet. Or half a mile of girders."

"It sounds like you started out in construction work."

"I did."

"From there . . . to all those Ransom buildings," she murmured. "That took some doing. It never happens 'just like that,' does it?" He really was quite a person, she reflected.

"It sure doesn't." His sharp eyes warmed up some more. "But you know, all those buildings, end to end, don't add up to one of your little statues. I envy you that."

There it was again, that peculiar wistfulness. "You shouldn't," she protested. "Think of all the people who have a decent place to live in the housing projects. Your projects are the best and most beautiful in the country, Nick."

"They have to be." His tone was sober. "They're my . . . special commitment. When I was a kid my family was thrown out of our house, you see. And there were six of us."

"Good heavens, how horrible," she exclaimed.

"I've never forgotten it," he admitted. "It's something my . . . that other people could never fully understand."

Amy wondered, "My" what?

"*I* do," she said with quick empathy. "When I was a child I remember hearing my mother talk about 'making the rent.' That was always the biggest worry. Maybe that's why my loft means so much to me." She was slightly embarrassed at having revealed so much of herself, even though Nick had reciprocated.

"You understand a lot of things," he said softly, and there was a brilliant gleam in those light, penetrating eyes.

Suddenly she wondered if this whole thing was just a device for seduction, tailored to her own personality. Maybe associating with Jeff had made her cynical; it had certainly made her wary. And it was certain that a man like Nick Ransom, shrewd and determined enough to come to everything from nothing, would know which notes to play. The idea disturbed and saddened her, took some of the edge of brightness from their interval.

Amy glanced at her watch. It was almost ten. "It can't be," she said involuntarily.

Nick looked at his watch, too. "No, it can't," he agreed, giving her another of his sharp, searching glances.

"I really must go. I have a busy day tomorrow. And you said you have to leave town . . ."

He looked taken aback for a second, then he said casually, "Not until late afternoon."

"Neither of us is on a human schedule." She smiled to lighten the sudden air of tension, and got up. "I'll just go and compliment the chef."

Nick was on his feet at once, and she felt him staring after her when she went out to the kitchen, thinking how much she liked this house. And Nick Ransom. But she couldn't afford to like him too much, to get trapped into another emotional disaster.

"I hope you come back to see us," Kim said,

giving her his crinkly smile. He'd been very flattered when she'd asked him about his painting.

She smiled back but didn't promise. It might be better not to come back. Strange how much that decision depressed her.

Nick watched Amy and her Scottie enter the street door of the loft building. He found himself wishing she lived in a busier neighborhood, but at least her building was secure. His practiced eye had registered that right away.

He drove off thinking about her. She'd felt good at the cabin, it was clear. And he liked the way she'd talked to Kim—as a fellow artist, not a servant, the way Janet inevitably would have.

And Nick remembered how beautiful her eyes and her hair had been by candlelight. But the eyes were mistrustful, still. If she only knew it, the last thing in the world he'd ever do was hurt her. As that spoiled, rich turkey, Windom, must have hurt her.

She was still reacting to that, Nick was sure.

Or maybe he just didn't turn her on. It was a lousy conclusion, but it might be the right one. Maybe he was just her employer, somebody she had a few things in common with. He could never compete with Golden-Boy Windom and his damned Ivy League education, his snooty family.

One thing was sure. Amy didn't give a damn about money. Otherwise she would never have run away from Windom. And money was the best thing Nick had to offer. Janet had told him so ten thousand times, and he'd started to believe her.

When he let himself into his condo, it looked like a mausoleum.

The phone was ringing.

"Ransom." He answered without enthusiasm.

"Nick, Rod."

Sprawling into a futuristic leather chair, Nick got a cigarette out of a box of polished steel. "What's up?"

"Nothing's *up*." Rod sounded disgruntled. "My stocks are falling."

Whose aren't? Nick asked in sardonic silence. He'd had a strong feeling when he dropped Amy off that he was going to have to slow down, keep his distance, or scare her off for good. "Swell. Specifically?"

Rod gave him specifics. "If you want me to hang up my jock, you've got it," Rod summed up.

"Come off it, Wales. I didn't wrap it up, either . . . remember? Tell you what, I'll fly up there tomorrow afternoon. Maybe we can come up with something different."

"Okay. But I feel like I'm not earning my keep."

Nick retorted with a rude expression, consulted an airline schedule by the phone and told Rod when he'd arrive.

He hung up and leaned back in the chair, putting his feet on the leather ottoman.

The Windoms were something else. But damn it, he was going to talk them around. Now he had more reason than ever. They'd held him up longer than anyone ever had in his whole career.

And their son had played hell with Amy Hill.

He had to be rotten, or she'd never have left

him. She was the loyal type. He'd found that out from a conversation they'd had, on the way back to town. They'd gotten on the subject of childhoods again; something she let slip tipped Nick that her father had been a boozer. She'd tried to cover it up, anxious not to condemn the man. She was damned loyal; it would take a lot to make her throw in the towel.

But maybe it was the Windom *family* that had gotten to her. Nick hadn't considered that before, and the idea ate at him. Yes, maybe it was Jeff Windom's family she couldn't take, not the man himself. Nick felt another burning jab of jealousy, like a knife-point in his solar plexus.

When he was packing for the Boston trip, he suddenly laughed out loud. There was one consolation: Rod had made an honest man of him. Now he *was* going out of town.

He'd been lying through his teeth when he told Amy he was. The ploy, giving him a chance to see her, had been irresistible.

It was a good thing he was leaving. He'd never gotten anywhere with lying and he was sure she was the kind who hated being lied to. But in this case, he told himself, it had been a kind of equivocation—the all's-fair syndrome.

She'd had a good time with him this evening, he knew that. When she could let herself, poor kid. Amy had been burned so bad she'd jump now if anybody lit a match.

Then he remembered something else: she'd changed the dog-group, added her Scottie and two Dobies. Nick was no shrink, but that had to mean something. Something nice—like the Scottie and the Dobies and the mutt were a kind of family.

His spirits shot up. He'd waited for someone like Amy for thirty-nine years. He'd waited for the Windom land, too. And he was going to win them both. Even if he had to go on "equivocating" until the last toot on the horn.

Even if he had to use maneuvers that would make Machiavelli look like George Washington.

That resolve calmed him enough so he could zero in on the next step with the Windoms—the people who'd thrown the Ransoms to the wolves more than thirty years before.

CHAPTER FIVE

"That's *just* right!" Amy said to George, the mold maker. He beamed at her. The mold had been made in the thinness of cloth, allowing for instant re-creation of the form and dress of the girl with the ball. The exuberant clay child, Amy thought, represented the child she herself had never had time to be.

Now the wax would go to wax-working, then to the ceramic-shell department, where the wax would be burnt out and molten metal poured over the shell. Accustomed to the sights, smells, and sounds of a working atelier, Amy was in her element. It was real artistic pleasure working with something that changes as it is reproduced first in one material, then another.

"I guess that's it then," she said to George. "Now who do I see about the patina?" The patina, or finish, was a very critical matter.

"Harold Landau, Ms. Hill. I'll show you where he is."

They were going out to the hall when Amy saw Langella. The mold man greeted him with great respect. Langella hugged Amy. "Where's the corpus delicti?" he demanded.

"Right behind us. Want to autopsy it?" Amy shot back.

With a typical, curt nod Langella walked her back into the room. He stood surveying the dancerlike figure of the child. Amy held her breath.

Langella walked around the figure, squinting at it fearsomely from every angle.

Finally he said, "Yes. Absolutely."

That was his highest seal of approval. Amy was so happy she could feel the quick tears in her eyes.

"You look like you've been through the wringer, girl," Langella said bluntly. "Come on, let's get you some coffee."

"I've got to see Mr. Landau about the patina—"

"In a minute. You can spare your senile old teacher that, can't you?" Langella chuckled, his black, sharp eyes belying the adjectives.

She gave a ridiculing hoot. "I think I can."

When they were sitting in the artists' lounge, he asked, "What are you using, your Byzantine blue?" She nodded. "You know it's not my cup of tea, but in this case I think you're right on target."

He smiled at her. "Let me tell you something, lady. You've caught a . . . quality in this one *and* the dogs that I've never seen you catch before. It may sound cruel, and I hope you won't take it that way, but it seems to me the Boston fiasco did something good for you. You've shot up like a weed, creatively speaking."

"I'm anything but offended, maestro. How could I be?"

"But you've been working like someone possessed," Langella exploded. "If I can stick my nose in again, I think you'd better take a little break before you start the lovers. I'd hate to see you suffer from burnout, Amy."

She knew what good advice that was. Her whole body was blurred from exhaustion. She admitted as much to Langella.

"I've been on such a roll," she confessed, "I couldn't take a breather between the dogs and the girl."

She'd shelved everything for the duration of the creative fever, working so obsessively she'd fallen asleep every night like a stone. She hadn't given Jeff a thought, hadn't even worried about a recurrence of the horrible publicity.

The work had been all-consuming, making Amy feel she'd seen the end of a disastrous chapter in her life, and the start of a whole new one. It had made her utterly free.

Free of Nick Ransom, too, she began to believe as the rich, crowded hours and days sped by. She hadn't heard from him for weeks. That gave her a slight twinge, and yet she told herself it was just as well; a troublesome door had closed before it even opened. She'd been able to give all her attention to the pieces, pour all her passionate emotion into them.

But now Langella was waiting. She realized she hadn't given him a real answer about taking a break.

"I will. I promise," she said. "A week, maybe."

But after he'd left, and she'd finished her conference with the patina expert, Amy shortened the avowed week to two lazy days.

The next night she knew that one had been enough: already the figure of the lovers nagged at her consciousness. Assistants had already built the armature. Chandler had one of the housing project's outdoor benches sent to the loft, so she could get the proper feeling. Inspired by her other idol, Jamison, Amy planned to sculpt the lovers' figures so they could be seated on an actual bench duplicated in concrete.

With new enthusiasm and a high heart, she began on the young adults' bodies and progressed to the responsive tilt of heads. The faces would come last.

She had envisioned them in a tender half-embrace: there would be nothing blatant or offensive in the expression of their emotion; yet they must suggest, at once, discovery, wonder, and commitment.

For one dreadful moment she panicked—what qualified her to delineate love's wonder? Her only love had been nothing but illusion. Failure.

She wished she had chosen any other subject under the sun. This statue could reflect her failure in its own.

The dogs had been so easy . . . and the child. That was because she knew and loved dogs more than almost anything in the world; she knew the half-formed, naïve hopes of children, perhaps, because she still had not become a full woman.

The idea was so daunting, so depressing that it nearly paralyzed her for half a day. But with her stubborn temperament she persisted, even if the work had turned slow and hard and agonizing.

It was the woman's face she was most unsure of. She hoped her uncertainty would not show itself in the shadow-woman's features. Right now, she decided, she would just have to postpone the forming of them; start on the man's.

When she began she found she was having difficulty with his face, too. She wanted to make it . . . older. Always instinctive rather than analytical, she didn't question why.

The phone sliced into her muddled reflections, making her jump. She might as well answer, for all the good she was doing in her studio. Before she picked it up, she glimpsed herself in a mirror: her eyes looked huge and dark-shadowed, her face thinner, and she realized she hadn't looked at herself critically—beyond a clean face and tidy hair—for days. She must have lost five pounds.

Distractedly she picked up the receiver and answered with a brief, inhospitable hello.

"Amy?"

Hearing Nick Ransom's voice again, after so long, had an amazing effect. She felt an unexpected pleasure, something bordering on excitement. Her own reaction stymied her.

"Amy? It's Nick."

"I know," she said unsteadily. "How are you?"

"Back where I belong, thank God. It seems like . . . a long time since we've spoken." He sounded as if his calm were an effort. "I don't want to disturb you—I know you've been working awfully hard. I just had to tell you that I've seen the statues. They're beautiful. Beautiful." The steady voice wavered, so little that only her sensitive ear could perceive it.

She answered and her voice was pitched a bit higher than usual, "Thank you." And she heard herself add, "I need some encouragement today. This third one is a"—she groped for a light word —"toughie."

"I'm sorry to hear it. Maybe you need to relax," he went on quickly. "Do you think a concert, say . . . and dinner, would help any?"

She made a sudden decision. "No. Not 'any' . . . a *lot.*"

There was a quick intake of breath on the line, relief when he said, "I'm glad I waited for the rest of that. Wonderful. We'll keep it casual and I'll pick you up at six."

She was surprised to discover how much she did look forward to the evening. This was as unexpected as her reaction when she heard his voice. She admitted to herself that she'd actually missed him—missed his strong, soothing presence, his compatible company. She'd been an idiot to make so much of his interest in her; to be so skittish. He was not another Jeff Windom, in any way. He was an intelligent, attractive man she liked being with and who liked being with her. She decided to make no more of it than that.

Amy dressed casually in a burnt-orange sundress that had its own long plaid jacket. It flattered her faint tan and dark coloring, and also disguised a little her new thinness. She arranged her hair softly to blur the planes of her hollowed cheeks.

It was almost six before she remembered to check her supplies; she never ran much of a bar, in any case, but was pleased to discover she had some bourbon left over from a previous party, recalling that Nick had chosen that drink at the cabin.

When his ring came—to the minute—she couldn't help a flashback to Jeff's cavalier attitude toward timing. She liked the opposite in Nick. Very much.

He was smiling widely; there was an extraordinary warmth and brightness in his sharp eyes, and he was wearing a gray denim suit whose easiness could not disguise its perfect fit. The clothes emphasized the pitch-blackness of his neat, short hair, the startling contrast of those penetrating eyes.

"It's so good to see you." She thought how strange it was that each time she saw him, she felt as if they'd known each other for years.

He held out a flat, rectangular package, stunningly wrapped in gift paper printed with golden dragons that matched its golden ribbon. "I picked this up for you in Japan," he said lightly.

"How nice! Please . . . sit. Can I get you a drink? Bourbon and water?"

He continued to stand, studying her from head to foot. He looked inordinately pleased. "You've got a great memory . . . on top of everything else. Thanks, I wouldn't mind one."

When she came back with his drink and her ever-present iced coffee, Mischief was trotting along, having just finished his dinner.

Nick took his drink and squatted down to pet the Scottie. "Hiya, kid! How ya *doin'?*"

"So you were in *Japan,*" she said.

"Oh, yes." Nick got up and sat down beside her on the couch. His response had been a little weary. "*And* Boston, New York, Oregon, and California." He blew out his breath. "And *damned* glad to be back." The gray eyes stayed on hers for an instant. "Of course, there are nice things in Japan."

That recalled her to the gift. "May I?" she smiled, tearing away the wrapping. She exclaimed. It was an exquisitely printed picture book on Japanese snow sculpture.

"Oh, this is marvelous! Do you believe that's one of my favorite subjects?" She leafed through the book avidly. "The way they take a disastrous blizzard, and turn hard luck into something so beautiful." She held out the book, calling his attention to a particular photo—pure-white, carved figures of big, mythical-looking creatures.

"It's amazing," he breathed. But he was looking at her, not the picture. "I mean, that idea of yours. That's the very thing that got to me. I watched some of the work being done, one very bad winter."

It was amazing, she thought, *how alike their ideas were.* The reminder made Amy feel irrationally shy, and once again she saw Nick as a man; was conscious of the strength of his big, square hands, the power in his shoulders and the wiry legs outlined by the snug denim trousers.

To break the rather awkward silence, she said

quickly, "Thank you for this. It's just beautiful, and I'm going to enjoy it."

He waved his hand dismissively. "Glad you like it. But never mind my travels, what about you? You must have been working like a beaver." His glance took account of her hollowed-out cheeks, swept over her thinner body. "I didn't hire you to kill you," he added.

She flushed. "It's always that way with me," she confessed. Then she amended, "Nearly always. I get so involved. I must admit this project is something special." She was feeling vulnerable again, open; moved by the real concern in his voice and his eyes.

"It certainly is." Their glances locked and held. She was the first to look away, and he seemed to recall himself. "What do you say we stuff you with Italian food?" He grinned. "Do you like it?"

"Love it."

He stood up. "Then *andiamo.*"

The restaurant was an expensive but cozy place whose decor recreated an Italian village, complete with casual tenors and mandolin music.

Nick kidded one of the tenors, who turned out to be a Jewish man from The Bronx, in New York, and the man answered him back in rapid-fire Yiddish.

"I won't translate that," Nick told Amy, laughing. The easy way Nick had with people charmed her. Jeff had always been so aloof and arrogant. "You just did."

"You're quick," he said approvingly as their drinks were delivered.

"Where I grew up you had to be." She gave him a salute with her glass.

There was a gleam in his eye. "I can relate to that." He returned the salute, and they drank. "I learned to run before I learned to fight."

She laughed. "So did I. I learned to sprint at department store sales. I was out of my weight-class, but I was very fast."

"That takes courage. Women at sales—I'd match them up against anyone at the Golden Gloves." He shook his head and grinned. "At least in my old neighborhood."

She could sense their unspoken words below the banter. His eyes kept admiring her; he looked so open that he made her feel open, too. The strong cocktail was hot and phosphorescent in her veins; after the work marathon, her emotions felt tender, exposed. She'd have to watch herself.

She looked away from him, suddenly became immersed in the huge menu. He noticed her change and quickly switched the talk back to himself, started telling her a funny story about his adolescence in Boston.

Amy thought, *Nick is exactly my kind of people.* As he poked fun at himself for her entertainment, Amy was aware of the bitterness below the humor. *Nick Ransom's past,* she thought, *was very much with him.* And she was aware of something else—his urgent magnetism. There was a seductive command in his light-gray eyes and she was disturbed by their power.

At the pop concert they went to after dinner, Amy could feel his nearness touch her, like fingers;

his massive presence was strangely consoling and familiar. Jeff had hated music like this. He'd always called it "elevator music," made fun of all her sentimental favorites.

Involuntarily she made a sound of exasperation, frowning. She'd be glad when she could forget Jeff Windom, once and for all.

"Something wrong?" Nick whispered. She caught his sidelong glance; she hadn't realized he'd been watching her.

She shook her head and smiled, looking back at the orchestra. But she could still sense his observation, the warmth of those gray and penetrating eyes.

When they went out to smoke at the intermission, he asked lightly, "Having memories?"

It was the first question he'd ever asked her that approached intrusion and it surprised her. But what surprised her more was her own reaction—she was feeling so warm toward him that she didn't mind at all.

He looked as if he regretted speaking, but his face cleared when she said calmly, "Only bad ones. Like a bad tooth."

He grinned, lighting her cigarette. "Then it's got to come out."

"I think it already has." If she'd been surprised before, now she was stunned. The "bad tooth" had, at last, been extracted. And she'd healed more quickly than she'd ever imagined. Thanks to Nick Ransom.

He certainly *wasn't* Jeff: she'd fallen head over heels for Jeff Windom the first minute she saw him. It had taken nearly three months to fall for Nick. And she'd been such a fool that she'd blithely assumed what she felt for Nick, therefore, was anything but love.

It was such a stunning realization, right there in the midst of the crowded lobby, coming with the lightning suddenness of summer rain, that she could only stare into Nick's eyes. Those eyes were blazing. He'd understood exactly what she meant, in those few ironic words.

Nick was speechless, too.

He just kept looking at her with his whole heart in the look, not able to glance away even when his cigarette burned his fingers. Wincing slightly, with his eyes still on her face, he dropped the cigarette into a receptacle, almost walking in his sleep when the end-of-intermission signal came.

His hand reached out for her arm, pressed it against his body as they walked side by side back into the concert hall, releasing her reluctantly when they had to part, moving in single file to their seats.

As soon as the lights went down again, his powerful fingers closed about hers, and he looked down at her with a blissful, worshiping face. His fingers, all of a sudden, felt very secure, as if she had stepped into a warm house, secure and solid to the rafters, and her sheltered, homecoming spirit answered with a tender, grateful pressure from her own captured fingers.

She could feel and see his quickened breathing, his hungry impatience. And she knew, even before it happened, that they had made a tacit agreement;

that soon they would rise, like one person, and leave the concert hall and hurry for the shadows of the car.

When at last they were inside it, he turned to her with cautious slowness, still not quite certain. But then he read her face and his eyes blazed to bright silver and he lowered his mouth to hers.

The kiss was more than she had ever known a kiss could be; more than any joy, both an answer and a declaration. It shook her to her depths. And opening softly under his, her mouth responded, saying every silent word that had been buried in her heart.

Free now to her wild pleasure, she let her questing hands discover the feel of his hard, massive neck, the planes of his face and the shape of his close-molded ears. Her sculptor's hands delighted in the contours of those powerful shoulders, the texture of his night-black hair.

She heard him gasp in delight, felt his strong hands trace her narrow shoulders, her arms, the slight curve of her figure and the form of her long, trembling thighs. He stopped her mouth again with his, and through closed eyes she glimpsed the scarlet and the silver splash of her heightened senses, her high, blind happiness.

He sat back, inviting her to lean against him, and whispered against her hair, "Do you know how long I waited, just to touch your hand? To have *this* . . ."

His arm squeezed her shoulder, drawing her closer to him as he kissed the top of her head. "This," he repeated, "I can't believe."

"Neither can I." She smiled against his chest. She'd thought it would take years to get over Jeff Windom. She was stunned with the sweet unexpectedness of this new emotion.

He stroked her arm. "You know when this hit me? The first time I saw you, in that car, on the expressway. Then I felt like grabbing you, right there on the plane."

She was overcome with tenderness, melting with it. He'd been so patient, so determined. She lifted her face; this caress was different, not so tender, more impatient.

She whispered, and her voice was shaky, "Take me home."

He was gently releasing his arm, then, starting the car, and they drove off swiftly toward the loft.

Amy watched his strong profile in the passing lights: she'd never seen his hard face look so happy.

When they walked in the loft, Mischief was sleeping on a big armchair. He wagged his stumpy tail, opened one eye and went back to sleep.

Nick took Amy in his arms. "That was the highest compliment. He acts like I . . . belong here." Nick's eyes smiled into hers.

"You do." She had the feeling he'd said that to give her more time, to ease her, as if he knew what a momentous thing this was.

But the seriousness of her answer made his gray eyes glisten even more. He grabbed her in his arms, kissing her with a starved and eager mouth, and she realized the desperation of his need.

And then abruptly she was tense, uncertain. Tonight had gone so fast; the tumultuous new feelings had come from nowhere, there in the lobby of the concert hall. Now, almost before she'd known what happened, they were in each other's arms.

Nick read her. He moved back, releasing her, and took one of her hands. "Talk to me," he said gently . . . she had never heard his voice so gentle . . . "there's so damned much to say."

She warmed with tenderness again. In this he'd never failed her, this incredible patience and understanding.

When they were sitting close together on the couch, he said, "You know, there must have been a thousand times when I had so much to say I was afraid to say anything at all. And I came up with nothing, or some dumb platitude."

Amy slid her hand under the hand that held her. He squeezed her fingers. Impulsively she bent over and kissed his hand, felt him tremble from the gesture.

"It's the damnedest thing," he murmured. "Talking to you like this is almost like making love."

Her heart was full. "It *is* making love."

His hard arm drew her close to him. When he spoke again, she felt his warm breath on her head. "I'd like to clear up some mysteries, while we're at it. The way I knew your dog's name. I really goofed on that one." And he told her all about it— his early "detective work," sending the leash, going to look at her sculpture.

Laughing softly, he admitted, "Imagine what I felt like when I saw what you could do. It was a whole new game, then. I knew you were the artist —as well as the woman—I'd been looking for. You must have wondered, when I kept maneuvering you into dinners . . ."

She nodded, grinning.

"Why I couldn't let someone else show you the model. All that. I had to bite my tongue when you mentioned your friend Rhoda. I nearly said, 'Sure. The one who stayed in your place while you were in Boston.' That would have blown it altogether. I was so damned afraid of scaring you off."

"You don't have to be afraid of that now."

It was true. Whatever doubts she'd had were gone, like the figures from a nightmare, in the light of morning.

There was nothing to be afraid of. Nick Ransom was not Jeff Windom, in any way at all.

Nick put his hand under her chin and tipped her face upward, staring into her eyes with deadly seriousness.

"I want you to be sure. As sure as I am. I want a lot more than just one night."

"I know. I *am* sure."

CHAPTER SIX

Tasting her sweet, giving mouth, holding her so tightly to him she was as near as the beat of his heart, Nick thought hazily, *This is like going over a waterfall.*

Yes. Now, instead of fighting the currents and the tides, as he had done all his life, he was flowing with them. Nothing had ever felt like this before, not with any woman. Going with the feelings, yet in full command—there had never been such power and such certainty in his body or his hands. Every sinew of him was alive: all the buildings and the money, the successes and the deals, were nothing, paltry stuff compared to the pulsing, living beauty that he possessed now with his astonished fingers.

She was so soft, her skin so satiny as she moved under his seeking hands. He exulted in her, discovering the small, rounded shoulders and silky arms, finding the shape of her generous breasts and that magical female curving from the waist to the long, delicious legs.

Nick raised his mouth, gasping, and looked down into her eyes—the big, brown eyes that always reminded him of a deer's. He saw that she felt it too and it was almost impossible to believe! She cared for him, Nick Ransom, or this would never be happening.

Easy, easy, he warned his raging senses—this must be right for her, right for them, perfect in every respect. He must bring to this, the greatest of his life's moments, an absolute perfection.

As gently as he knew how, Nick turned her in his grasp, guiding her steps toward the dimly lit bedroom he had glimpsed, and feeling her grace, matching the rhythm of his slow steps to hers, it was like they were dancers . . . or two enchanted people pacing toward a solemn rite, a stately wedding.

Amy moved with him almost in a dream, her own house grown dim and unfamiliar. The solemn weight of his gestures told her this was important to him, and knowing that, she longed to give to him as she never had given before.

Now they paused in the faint golden light, facing each other, and her passion-blurred eyes took their fill of his loving face with its strong, hard features; his black ruffled hair and his tenderly invading eyes, like molten pewter, gleaming into her own. She moved to him, into him, and his large hands were strangely gentle at the fastenings of her dress, sliding it off her shoulders, freeing her body of it until she stood before him in wisps of lace barely covering her.

He took a quick, sharp breath, seeing her almost naked beauty. Slowly, softly, he removed the first of the lacy fragments, stooping to lightly kiss her breasts. She shuddered at his touch, reaching out her hands to stroke his face.

But now he was sinking to his knees, sliding his big hands down her body, and she trembled even more as his fingers traveled down her legs and ankles to her sandaled feet. He was slipping off the sandals, stroking her naked legs again; his firm hands leisurely ascended, leisurely removed the other scrap of lace to free all of her for him. He said her name, wildly, again and again, and his passionate whisper sounded like the rubbing wings of butterflies, a steady, arousing, delicate rhythm.

She had never even dreamed of such joy, and such intense pleasure, spreading, burning, flooding from her center. She was quaking, climbing to a mad forgetfulness; quaking so she knew that she must crumble, but his massive hands locked her securely in her blind delight. Crying out she slid down in his hard embrace, feeling his big frame quiver with his unexpended need.

She took both his hands and began to rise, urging his clothes away with a newly brazen touch, until he stood before her naked too.

She saw his body with a wonder equal to his in observing hers. She had never seen such perfection. His massive shoulders loomed; his wide chest displayed a pleasing sparseness of dark, wiry hair, springing to her eager fingers, and his torso was as tough and solid as a tree. There was a panther line of leanness to his muscled thighs.

Now she was learning all of him, touching him with her ecstatic sculptor's hands, and he was lifting her, carrying her, laying her down on the bed, lowering his powerful body over hers. They were together.

His hands were stroking her once more, and the stroking aroused new waves of wild, astonished pleasure. She was rising again to a desire almost unbearable, as strong as his, and he was muttering low endearments into her hair, still stroking and caressing her. Her own fingers began to answer and her touch brought forth his cry. Now they were ascending together to a dazzled brightness; she rocked with the huge impact of his fulfilment, at once the tremendous aftershock of hers.

Afterward they lay in peaceful silence, both feeling languorous and melted.

His eyes, when they met hers, were heavy-lidded, the hard planes of his face all smoothed away. "Amy," he whispered. He pulled her to him, enclosing her in his arms. "If I could only say what . . . Amy, the things I thought before, just before . . . I don't know where they came from, and now they're gone."

"They came from love." She smiled and kissed his chest. "But we don't need them . . . not anymore."

She heard his wordless exclamation, felt him pulling her closer and still closer to him, drunk and dazzled with her happiness. "I know I love you, Amy. I have from the first damned minute."

"I love you. I don't think I knew what that meant, until now."

She could sense his joy, his gratified astonishment in the feel of his hands upon her. "I was

100

afraid that could never happen, after . . ." He stopped short.

She knew how much he needed to be reassured. Because of Jeff.

"You know something? I don't think I felt like a real woman before." She told him about her doubts with the statue of the lovers; looking at him, she saw a new expression on his face—totally happy, more secure. And she thought, *I've given him the ultimate gift.*

He lowered his head and kissed her passionately. "I've never been much of a . . . giving person." He stemmed her denial with a finger on her lips. "I haven't. I've been a taker. A go-getter," he added wryly. "I guess life made me that way."

"Well, it made me that way, too."

All of a sudden, out of nowhere came the memory of Rhoda's intense interest in Nick Ransom, her certainty that he was interested in Amy Hill. She giggled uncontrollably.

"What's all that about?" he demanded. "As a lover I must be hilarious."

She had a feeling he wasn't joking, not completely, and took his face in her hands to deny that with kisses.

"I was just thinking about what my friend Rhoda said, almost from Day One—that you were interested in more than my sculpture."

"Smart woman. How right she was." He looked very pleased.

"She even asked me about your ears."

"My *ears?* What the hell for?" Infected by

Amy's giggle, he started to laugh, too. "And what did you tell her—big and ugly?"

"Stop that. They're very good ears, and I should know. I'm a sculptor, remember?" She made a bold pass at his body, delighted with how at ease she was with him already.

"You've got me between a rock and a hard place. When you do that I don't want to talk about ears. But my curiosity's burning now."

He slid his hand over the curve of her hip.

She told him about Rhoda's preoccupation with astrology, her lecture on Capricorn ears; her insistence that Nick and Amy sounded very right for each other.

"I think I'm going to get along with Rhoda just fine. I owe her a present for giving me such good reviews." His tone was light but Amy heard a serious note.

"Amy, I wish I could *tell* you . . ." he began.

"We're not word people, Nick. We're hand people. We both think with our hands."

"That's so nice. I never thought of it that way before." He moved closer. "In fact, when I'm with you I think of things that never occurred to me in my life." She gloried in the feel of his muscular body pressed to hers.

"So we think with our hands, do we?" Now his voice had a wicked ring. "My hands are doing some thinking right now."

Stroking her skin, he illustrated what he meant.

Amy opened her eyes to the morning, felt Mischief's cool nose nudge her left shoulder. She smiled, reaching out her other hand. Nick's side of the bed was empty. The bedroom door was closed again.

She heard Nick's voice from the dining area, then another man's quiet voice and a faint commotion; the closing of the loft's front door.

The door parted and Nick strode in, looking vibrant and full of life. He was dressed in his denim suit again. "Good *morning.*" He sat down on the bed and kissed Amy, then fondled Mischief. "You, too, pal."

Nick observed Amy. "You look wonderful in the morning."

"I feel wonderful . . . *this* morning." His eyes thanked her. "What's going on out there?"

"Nothing special. Breakfast."

She stroked his face. "You didn't *cook* it?"

"*Cook* it?" He shook his head, laughing. "Not in *this* life. I had some sent in. Are you hungry?"

"Ravenous. Because I feel so good." She stroked his face, admiring its fine, hard planes.

"That's good." He hugged her close. "But if you keep doing that . . . and looking at me like that, you're not going to get any."

"Ten minutes," she promised, "after I feed the dog."

"That's taken care of." His glance slid over her bare shoulders, the curves of her below the pulled-up sheet.

"You're quite a fellow."

"You've had your warning," he teased her. He gave her one more hard hug and went out, whistling to Mischief.

Showered, lightly made up, she got into a pajama suit of yellow silk and matching sandals.

She found him in the dining area, drinking coffee, feeding bits of something to Mischief. The table was covered in flowered pastel linen and a dozen covered dishes. There was a huge centerpiece of daisies in her ivory bowl.

"Nick. What a gorgeous breakfast."

"It goes with you. Do you know that's my favorite color?"

"Second sight." He pulled out a chair for her. She thought, *He makes everything so festive, so special.* There were two kinds of omelets, tulip-cut melons, a fabulous display of croissants and danish.

After breakfast, while they were finishing their coffee, the doorbell rang.

"The cleaning-up crew," Nick said. "Take your coffee to the living room, honey. And we can talk about today."

While two deft men were clearing away the remains of breakfast, Nick joined her on the couch. He kissed her on the nose.

"What's the drill? Are you working today?"

"Believe it or not, no. I think it can wait a little while."

His face lit up. "That's wonderful. Can we spend the day together?"

"Of course we can."

She lit a cigarette and leaned back contentedly while Nick took care of the caterers. From the door she heard their fervent thanks.

"Where'll it be?" he asked her, when they were

outside a little later. "Maybe a museum . . . you can educate me."

"I don't know about the education, but a museum sounds fine."

They spent a couple of pleasant hours in the Art Institute, and lunched in the garden restaurant. There was a special exhibition of Oriental art, attracting both of them after Nick's recent trip to Japan. The museum store was nearby.

He said casually, "Let's take a look." He eyed the jewelry reproductions. Referring to an intricate necklace of pure gold, he murmured, "Nice. Try that on, why don't you?"

"Oh, but Nick . . . it's—"

"Please." He looked so eager, she agreed.

"Like it?"

"It's . . . exquisite."

"We'll take this," he said casually to the salesclerk. He hadn't looked at the tag or asked the price.

"Nick," Amy said quietly as they were leaving. "This is lovely. Thank you. But you don't have to buy me things."

"You don't know how happy it makes me." He took her hand. "I haven't had much chance to do this, for a long, long time."

When he suggested that they do a "little window-shopping," she didn't have the heart to spoil his enjoyment. He was like a small boy who wanted to show her something he'd made for her.

And one thing led to another, despite her intermittent protests—before she knew it, they were in and out of boutiques she'd never dreamed of pa-

105

tronizing. Once, when she asked him whether he liked a certain dress in turquoise or yellow, he said, "I like them both." And he insisted on buying both!

Once it had started, there was no holding him down. At one point he asked her, with an anxiety that moved her, "I'm not acting like a . . . show-off, am I? What the uppah crust would call 'vulgah'?" He parodied the Boston accent. She knew he was thinking about Jeff, comparing his own actions with a Windom's.

"Vulgar?" She squeezed his arm. "I've never had such a good time in my whole life. You're like the prince in the fairy tale. We're two of a kind, remember—for you, it was the docks, for me it was the sales." She smiled at him and watched his face light up again.

"I remembered that, Amy. It made me want to give you everything."

"I love you for that. But I think you already have . . . and it isn't something we could buy in a store."

His eyes gave her all the answer she needed. But he said, "Just one more place. Please?"

Shaking her head, she gave in. They entered an elegant jewelry store, as hushed and velvety as a chapel.

Nick was far from awed. He asked her, grinning, "Are you like the girl in the movie, the one who said 'diamonds are tacky'?"

"You could hardly say that about these," she murmured. They were standing before a display of gold and diamond jewelry. Nick gestured to the hovering assistant, who removed a velvet tray from the case to show them.

At Nick's gentle insistence, Amy chose a pin and bangle bracelet; then, when he prodded, earrings that looked like twinkling stars.

"What about Rhoda?" Nick inquired. "I meant it when I said she needed a present. You said she's interested in astrology." He consulted the assistant, who showed them remarkable pins of gold with the various constellations in diamonds.

Amy decided on a white-gold pin with the Pisces constellation for Rhoda, and they had it gift-wrapped.

He glanced at his watch. "Damn it, I can't believe the time. I've got to go, darling. I've got some out-of-town people to take to dinner, but could I see you later. Maybe nine?"

"I'll be waiting."

Before he put her in a taxi Nick kissed her soundly, indifferent to everyone around them, as if the city belonged to them. Amy thought she saw a quick flash of light from somewhere, but told herself as the cab drove away, *I'm dizzy, that's all, from everything that's happened. My eyes are playing tricks on me.*

At home, she started receiving the deliveries. Taking garment after garment from their boxes, she could hardly believe how much he'd made her buy. It was like a dream—all this from a man who also gave her so much love. Nothing in her whole life could equal last night's perfection, and this perfect day.

She decided to meet Rhoda for an early dinner and take the gift to her.

But the gift would reveal what had happened: maybe it was too soon to tell her? On the other hand, she couldn't wait to give the gift.

She took a deep breath to steady her voice, and called. Rhoda was overjoyed to hear from her—she'd considerately left Amy alone during her marathon of work—and they made a date to meet.

Amy happily debated which new thing to wear, opting for a cool black jersey suit with a golden-yellow tank top. It was smashing with the museum necklace and the diamond-studded bangle.

When Amy arrived, Rhoda was already seated and looking as fresh as a garden in a lilac-colored dress. Her blue eyes lit up when she saw Amy. She got up and hugged her.

"What's happened to you?" she demanded in a breathless voice. "You're glowing. And that *suit* . . . everything!"

"It's a short and unbelievable story."

Amy told it.

Rhoda was silent, wide-eyed for a moment. "I . . . I don't know what to say. Except that it's marvelous. And high time. You deserve it, Amy. I'm just so happy for you I could explode."

"*Please* don't, not yet," Amy teased her. "You'll miss the rest."

"The *rest?* You've got to be kidding."

Amy took the gift from her bag and handed it to Rhoda. Puzzled, Rhoda unwrapped the jeweler's box, read aloud from a tiny card scribbled in Nick's jagged writing. "Thanks for the plug. N.R."

Rhoda looked at the beautiful pin and gasped. "The man is a fantasy. He couldn't be real."

"He's real all right," Amy said softly.

When she got back to the loft, she rushed into the studio to look at the uncompleted figures of the lovers—now there was no more uncertainty about them, no more doubt or fear.

She knew exactly what the expressions on those faces would be.

And she knew that she could capture those expressions; knew it more surely than she had ever known anything before.

"Bad luck you can't join us, Ransom." One of the visiting Englishmen, Selden, shook Nick's hand. "Been jolly interesting talking to you."

"Same here," Nick lied politely. It had been a "jolly" bore and he was impatient. Besides, he wasn't at all sure he was interested in the enterprise. All he could think of was the night before and the terrific afternoon. "Sorry about that commitment. But you couldn't have a better tour guide than Rod here."

He noticed Rod's curious glance; this was the first time he'd bowed out of entertainment. He'd always enjoyed it before, in a kind of detached fashion.

"Enjoy yourselves," he added, glad to see them go.

He dialed Amy's number, a little antsy when he heard five rings. His heart hammered against his ribs when she answered; her voice sounded absent, far away.

"Amy . . . darling?"

"Oh, *Nick.*" He relaxed. The warmth was back in her voice and its low sweetness stroked him.

"Are you busy?"

"Yes. I'm sorry I took so long. I was working on the lovers. I'm clay from top to bottom." Now she sounded buoyant.

"I'll take you any way I can get you. Can I still come over?"

"I couldn't stand it if you didn't."

His morale shot up like mercury and stayed there. "Why don't I give you some time . . . about an hour?"

He heard his own voice, usually hard as concrete, go all soft. It always did when he talked to her. "Okay?"

"Very okay. I'll be here."

He hung up, leaning back in his tall leather chair, gazing out over the glittering skyline of Chicago. Maybe that's why he'd urged those diamonds on her today—they reminded him of city lights.

"I'll be here," she'd said.

Amy was the kind of woman who would be there when she said she would.

He had an ugly flashback to a scene with Janet, his ex-wife. Nick shook his head. She was the only person in the world who'd ever put anything over on Nick Ransom. She'd seemed so sweet, so crazy about him. Then, almost as soon as they were married, the mask had come off. Not all at once; layer by layer. She'd even lied about liking dogs.

Nick could see his ex-wife's pretty, pouting face as clearly as if she stood before him.

He'd come home from an occasion like tonight's, left early to be with her. She always complained so when she had to go to social-business functions that Nick had stopped asking. Entering their penthouse, he'd been dismayed to see she was still out.

A few hours later she strolled in, wearing a short, shiny dress cut almost down to her navel. "Hello," she said briefly and went to the bar to mix a drink. She looked as if she didn't need it, he decided sourly.

"Where the hell have you been?" he demanded, more sharply than he intended.

"I'm not one of your hardhats, Ransom. Don't bellow at *me*." Calling him by his last name was a habit of hers when she was irritated and he hated the habit; it made her sound so tough. It annoyed him that a woman from such a ritzy background could talk as rough as any of his men.

"Well?" He controlled his voice. This wasn't the first, second, or third time this had happened. Lately she'd always been late, and never gave an explanation.

"I had a cocktail date with Sandra. She didn't show."

Nick doubted that her date had been named Sandra, or any other feminine name. But it was getting so he didn't care that much anymore; there was too much unpleasantness between them.

Her condescending way with his mother and brothers, her nasty little remarks about his background. At first she'd found his "tough-guy" persona very "titillating," as she put it.

He was beginning to see that it was the Ransom bank account that titillated her, long after he'd ceased to.

"That's very inconsiderate of . . . Sandra," he said ironically that night.

"What's that supposed to mean?" she retorted. "What do you expect me to do—sit around here all night waiting for you? I have some big choice. Either that, or go to one of those boring affairs. They're just like you, Nick. Boring, boring, boring."

Well, she hadn't been bored much longer. Not long after that she'd asked for a divorce so she could marry her cocktail date, whose name turned out to be Bill.

Janet had never been more than a spoiled little girl. And yet when he'd tried to spoil her in the early days of their marriage, she'd had a damping way of making him feel he was "gauche"—her pet word—and "vulgar."

That was another reason—besides Windom—he'd felt so unsure of himself today. Amazing how the past kept haunting you.

Amy's past might be haunting her, too. He was going to have to give her time to forget the bad old days.

Now, though, their days promised to be good. Very good. Better than he'd ever hoped for. Nick thought of all the amazement, the pleasure, the crazy happiness of the last wonderful night and day.

Amy made everything beautiful and made him feel she cared.

He was going to be damned careful this time. Careful to remember that Amy wasn't Janet. Amy was like no other woman in the world; she was just herself. A woman with a gift that made her a person in her own right, as poor Janet had never been.

And he was going to have to watch his idiotic jealousy, keep the Windom episode out of his mind.

It was almost time to leave; he wanted to stop and get her something. But what?

What was that poem Rod quoted? Something about wine and roses. Easy—he'd take her a carload of roses and the oldest damned wine he could find.

And maybe something for the dog.

CHAPTER SEVEN

Amy walked around the figure of the lovers, checking it from each perspective. From every angle it was strong and eloquent. She couldn't believe she'd made so much progress in a week.

She couldn't believe the *week,* as far as that went. These seven days with Nick Ransom had transformed her world.

From the studio door, Mischief let out an impatient bark. "Okay. I know." She floated down to earth.

She had to go out for dog food, or Mischief wouldn't have any dinner.

She washed up, jammed keys and money into her pockets and went out to the supermarket.

Standing in the checkout line, she glimpsed the hateful masthead of the *Last Word,* trying to ignore its usual screaming headline.

But she couldn't. History was repeating itself.

This one shouted NEW COMBO—SWINGING SCULPTOR, TOUGH-GUY TYCOON.

She stared at a photo of herself and Nick, kissing good-bye outside the jewelry store. *That's* what the flash had been.

Amy moved forward in the line, with a slight feeling of nausea; the perspiration broke out on her skin underneath the heavy jumpsuit, and her heart was racing.

The checkout clerk was not one she knew, thank heaven. Amy avoided the girl's eye, waiting for change and the packing. But the girl, when she handed Amy change, said excitedly, "Hey, wow! You're Amy Hill." Chattering as she packed the cans into the bag, the girl rattled on: "I'm going to tell everybody I waited on somebody *famous*. You have a nice day."

Amy managed a frozen smile and fled.

When she unlocked the loft door, she heard the phone shrilling. For a second she decided not to answer. But it might be Nick. She picked up the receiver.

It was. "Amy?" He spoke before she could even answer.

"Yes?"

"I can tell from your voice. You've seen that rag." He sounded furious.

"Yes."

"I'm sorry. Are you okay, honey?" After she murmured another yes, he went on, "I was ready to fly to New York and break up their office." His tone was more relaxed now, self-mocking, and it made her smile. "But Rod, and my lawyers, dissuaded me."

"Good." She felt almost the way she had when she'd seen that first awful story, unsure of whether to laugh or cry.

"You sound better."

115

"I am."

"I'm glad, darling." She heard him take a deep breath before he said, "I was all wound up, planning invasion of privacy suits, about a million other attacks, but the lawyers are convinced that would only make it worse. Their advice is to just let it die a natural death. And I think it will—we're not going to create enough scandal to make it worthwhile. I want you to hang on to that, Amy."

"I'll try. But Nick, why can't they let it *alone* . . . why do they keep on? I've never been a headliner, and—"

She stopped short. But Jeff Windom and his family were; so was Nick Ransom.

"But you are," she amended.

"I guess I am. I've always driven the media nuts because I'm so closemouthed. There's another thing. They're probably lashing out from sheer frustration." His tone expressed disgust.

"What do you mean?"

"They haven't been able to dig up any dirt on you. You can bet they've checked you out back to your birth certificate, and haven't found anything juicy, to pad the Boston story. Now they're just reaching."

"I see." Maybe he was right. Maybe the thing would die of attrition.

"I think that's the way it'll be, Amy. Look, I hate it for you—and *my* frustration is that I can't just take 'em all out of the play."

He sounded so fierce that it set off her laughter. "My hero."

"Now, that's more like it. I've got to go, darling. See you for dinner. Believe me, it's going to be all right. Everything's going to be fine."

When she hung up, she was ready to believe him.

Even more so that evening, when he took her to a very special dinner.

And, as the succeeding nights and days passed without disturbance, she concluded that it had all been much ado about nothing. They'd live it down.

The *Last Word* was living up to its name.

Autumn had always been Amy's favorite time, and this year, as it approached, it was glorious.

Evenings and weekends, which had been so lonely, had turned to treasures. Apart from that first day of their spending spree—they called it The Binge—their weekdays were crowded. Amy had never been so busy or so happy, devoting her days to finishing the lovers or a rare lunch with Rhoda or one of her museum friends.

The nights and weekends were hers and Nick's; no matter how clay-stained or punchy she was from work it was a matter of discipline to greet him scented and shiny-haired, wearing soft lounge clothes when they were staying in or sleek and polished when they were going out.

With the swift passage of every night and day, she seemed to hold her happiness like an almost overflowing cup of precious liquid of which she feared to spill a single drop. Nick was the most perfect man for her that she could ever imagine. All of her life was so splendid it was hard to believe it could last. Now and then she would say to herself, *I've got to wake up, and he'll be gone.*

But magically, she didn't, and he wasn't, night after night and day after day.

They divided their time among the several residences, staying at the cabin mostly on weekends. Nick loved the loft, she discovered to her tender amusement, more than any place of his. When he took her to his condo, she'd been dazzled by its luxury and almost sci-fi gimmicks on the one hand, a bit daunted by its slickness on the other. He frankly referred to it as just a phony stopover, touchingly eager to have her make improvements and suggestions that would make it, he said, a "place to *live.*" She promised that as soon as the lovers were finished she would, and in the interim suggested a few small things which he quickly followed up on. She was pleased to notice that even those minor changes gave the condo a warmer feeling.

In the long, close evenings he'd told her a great deal about himself—his tough initiation to the Boston streets as a child, the sparse schooling, the long, grinding hours of work on the docks and in construction; his beginnings as a contractor and builder, and the astonishing rise to the head of Ransom. Her head whirled with the stories of the politics and "deals," the daring of his manipulations.

Through all of it, there was an unbroken and shining thread of honesty and courage, of unique imagination. She discovered more and more that Nick was a very complex man. Even his speech, his thought processes, alternated between the hardhat and the frustrated artist. He had a very real longing to enter more into her world, and she loved showing him the way.

"In a funny way," he said once in a confiding moment, "I guess making money's my art, the way your sculpture is yours. Crazy as that may sound."

"It doesn't at *all!*" They were lying in bed, and she moved to him, hugging him. "I read a marvelous poem once, something about the 'slant of light' at a certain time of the afternoon, on Fifth Avenue, in New York. The poet said if it hadn't been for the Rockefellers, the buildings wouldn't have stood just that way, creating just that slant of magical light."

She stroked his hair. "If it weren't for your special 'art,' there wouldn't be those wonderful places for people to live . . . or all these other beautiful buildings. I wouldn't have treasures out of Ali Baba's cave," she teased him affectionately . . . "or a place to put my statues."

He'd held her close to him then, and kissed her with a new fervor. "Ever since I've known you," he whispered, "there hasn't been a single time when you haven't said exactly what I needed to hear, Amy. The thing that makes everything right."

Those words always seemed so insignificant to her that she found his eternal gratitude almost shaming. So she said lightly, "It's the least I can do for the Lord Bountiful."

He still brought her something every single day, as if she were a child and the year was one long

Christmas. On top of the Binge's treasures, there'd been dozens of others—an exquisite pale mink jacket, after she remarked once that the nights were getting chilly; a small diamond Scottie for her lapel, another TV set for the bedroom so she wouldn't have to move her portable. It was endless, overwhelming.

She was fascinated, too, with his way of taking every luxury so for granted. It would be a while, she decided, before she'd get used to expressing the slightest wish and having it granted at the snap of his fingers. Once when she said it might be fun to have hot dogs for dinner, and started to cook some, he said, "Over my dead body. Relax. I'll take care of it." He went to the phone and in a half-hour an order of chili dogs, with every possible accessory, was delivered from the city's best Tex-Mex restaurant.

"Your time is precious," he said. "Not like . . ." he hesitated. "I was married before, Amy. We got divorced years ago." In a restrained way he told her what his former wife had been like. She'd been unfaithful over and over, once even with one of his friends.

Amy began to understand another source of his unease about Jeff, his occasional discomfort when she even acted friendly to Rod Wales. She knew it was because Rod had a lot in common with Jeff. There was one thing, though, Nick was never jealous of. And that was her work. Nick made it clear that he not only understood, but valued her for being an artist.

It was in this blissful state that Amy saw the

lovers casted. Langella said it was the finest thing she'd ever done, kidding her that this "sublimation idea was baloney," she'd been able to do it because she *wasn't* sublimating.

She was looking forward to the project opening, which would take place near the end of October. They were having perfect autumn weather: the sky was cobalt blue over the city, the sun pure golden. Amy had already planned what she would wear— a spirited new wool suit in cheerful pumpkin color, with a beautiful pin of golden-orange honey topaz that Nick had given her "for October." And, if the weather got colder, the silky mink jacket.

Even though the days grew nearer to the unveiling, it still felt like a dream.

When the day finally arrived Nick Ransom had never felt so good in his life, sitting there on the platform in the sun next to Amy.

He'd enjoyed seeing her eyes light up when she saw the three covered forms at center stage—her pieces. She'd supervise their placement tomorrow, had agreed with Nick that it would be fun to unveil them all at once like this.

Half-hearing the politico's usual harangue, Nick glanced at Amy. That color she was wearing made her hair and eyes look gorgeous, with a burnish like the bronze . . . soft and steady.

He'd feel even better later on, when he did what he'd been burning to do, all along.

Nick came to attention. It was time for him.

He got up and went to the mike on the lectern. Crumpling up the PR baloney they'd done for him at the office, he just started talking, looking at the faces of the people from the project; faces like his father and mother's, like his relatives', like his own.

Once he thought he heard a distinctive "Bull." He went right on, though, noting it seemed to come from a group of reporters with cameras, not the TV section.

He wound it up quickly—he never spoke more than five minutes to any collection of people. Then, with enormous pride, he introduced the sculptor Amy Hill.

He nearly exploded with pride, watching people's reaction to her. She spoke even more briefly than he had, arousing smiles when she said, "What I have to say is in these figures. And I hope you like them."

She pulled the cords that unveiled the three remarkable statues—that great one of the dogs, as if they were so happy they were dancing; the little girl with the ball, which for some unknown reason put a knot in his throat; and, in the center, the statue of the lovers sitting on the bench.

Amy had captured a feeling there that bowled Nick over. There was something about the way the woman looked up at the man that reminded him of the way Amy looked at him.

The whole assembly burst into applause, and Nick watched her beautiful face flush with pleasure, her big, soft eyes getting shiny.

That was it, then. The band started playing, and everyone was starting to mill around, congratulating him, congratulating Amy. He saw Rhoda Silver approaching with Rod Wales.

"I see you've met," Nick smiled.

"We have, indeed," Rod said, with an appreciative glance at Rhoda. "We've been reminiscing about Dixie."

Nick laughed, feeling even better. He thought, *Wouldn't it be something if our best friends got together?* He headed for Amy, waiting patiently until she could escape her fans and, bending over, gave her a quick kiss.

"You were terrific."

"So were you." Her wide smile flashed at him, her eyes bright as jewels. She looked on top of the world. Which was just where she belonged, where he was going to keep her, if he had to break his neck to do it. "Look, Nick, there's Rhoda."

Amy took his hand and they walked toward her friend, who was still with Rod.

A camera appeared from nowhere: there was a blinding flash, and a raucous male voice. "Give us a smile, Amy! You, too, Nick!"

Nick's hackles rose: What was this damned first-name business, anyway? The guy with the camera was grinning at them; he had a fat, foolish face, a thin little mustache.

"Get lost," Nick advised him.

"Come on, Nick, don't high-hat us. What's the word, for the *Last Word?*"

The paper's name hit Nick right between the eyes. And he had a strong feeling he was about to do some hitting, if this turkey didn't move. But the photographer wasn't too smart; he kept right on, aiming his camera. "One more shot, Amy. I want to get your decorations." His ferretlike eyes flicked over Amy's designer suit, her unique jewelry.

"Tell us about your sinecure," the reporter needled.

Sinecure. The word, with all its outrageous, untrue implications, lit Nick's fuse completely. This guy had a strong death wish, it seemed to him.

"I'm telling you again. Get lost." Nick grabbed at his camera and pulled: the strap was about to throttle him.

"Nick," Amy pleaded, putting her hand on his arm. He glanced at her swiftly, saw her pale, miserable face, and went a little mad. He grabbed the offensive reporter by his lapels and shook him.

"I'll charge you with assault!"

"Like hell you will." Now Rod was in it. "You'll charge *me,* you cockroach."

"Thanks anyway," Nick said to Rod. "I want this one myself." His words were so quiet that his sucker-punch took the reporter by surprise; Nick followed up with a fast combination to his gut and then took out the camera. Mister Dirty Word folded.

Flashbulbs popped; TV cameras were whirring.

Nick swore under his breath. He should have controlled himself, but the creep had sent him over the line.

Nick turned to Amy. She was shaking. "Come on, baby. Let's get out of here." He put his arm around her, moving her toward the parking area. Glancing back he saw Rod following, with Rhoda.

124

"Amy, are you okay? I'm sorry about the bout, but I couldn't let anybody talk to you like that."

"I'm all right." She tried to smile, but her mouth was shaky.

He touched her gently, signaling to get into the car. "Soon as we're celebrating, we'll forget it ever happened."

He got in and took her hand; it was cold in his. Her face looked . . . stiff. All the pleasure and light was gone from it.

My God, he thought. Maybe it was more than the punches. Maybe this thing has brought it all back—Boston, and the Golden Boy. Nick felt ice in the pit of his stomach. Maybe she was regretting she'd left Windom. It had to be something more than that little tussle. Otherwise, why should she look so devastated?

The idea was still eating at Nick when Rod and Rhoda got in the back, and Rod said lightly, "You do good work, Ransom." More gently, Rod asked, "How are you doing, Amy?"

"Fine, Rod." But Nick didn't believe it.

They fell silent as Nick drove them to the Cambria. He'd reserved a private room for their celebration. He thought Amy might like the gesture, since their first dinner had come from there. He watched her as they were escorted into the high-ceilinged sanctum with its mirrors and sculpture and flowers, and saw her remember.

"Will this do?" he asked her softly.

"It's perfect. Perfect that you remembered." When they were seated she took his hand. He began to feel better; she looked more like herself.

And yet there was something missing. He'd taken the shininess off her biggest day, and his spirits sank.

But he tried to enjoy it, so she could. He'd ordered the seven-course lunch, in small proportions, so the women could enjoy the flurry of service, all the little dishes.

Rhoda did, at least. She kept exclaiming over each new course. But it seemed to Nick that Amy was just trying to go along, to save his feelings.

The food was so visual he'd expected an artist to be delighted. Everything, even the calves' liver, was cut into flower petals. Amy said quietly, while the others were busy talking, "This is so . . . beautiful, after that other scene."

Nick glanced at the other two.

They were going on a mile a minute. They wouldn't be able to hear a word he said.

"You know I'd cut off my arm before I'd spoil anything for you," he said to her quietly. "And I felt like I'd spoiled your day for you." She looked at him with her big, soft eyes, and they were understanding but a bit puzzled. And he was afraid he saw something else in them—a kind of distance he hadn't seen before.

"But I told you before," he went on, "I couldn't let any man talk to you like that. You do understand that, don't you?"

"Of course I do. I love you for it. It was just so . . . ugly, Nick. As if no one is ever going to let us forget. Forget Boston." She flushed. "It wasn't just what happened; it was the idea that my past is some kind of 'dark star' "—her smile was sad and crooked—"that's going to keep on haunting us."

"That's crazy, honey," he protested.

He noticed that the others' talk had run out and sensed their observation. Amy did, too. She said quickly, "I think we should talk about this later."

And Nick could almost feel her effort to brighten up, not to dampen the party. He thought, damn the party, and everything else. It's her I'm concerned about. He didn't really believe it when she made a teasing remark to Rhoda about diets, getting another kind of talk started. He wanted just to be alone with Amy now, talk this thing out.

More than that, even, to see how she'd react to what he had in his pocket. If things had worked out according to Hoyle, he'd been planning to spring it on her right there at the table, in a covered dessert dish. It would have made it a *real* occasion.

Not now, though; somehow, the way it was now, it didn't seem the time. He cursed his own stupidity. He should have kept his cool.

When the other couple had to leave—Rhoda was in the midst of setting up a fashion show, and Rod had work to get back to as well—Nick heard the insincerity in his own "Don't rush."

He turned to Amy with a smile and took both her hands in his. "Let's talk. Where shall we go . . . the Art Institute?"

He knew she liked the garden there, and it might calm her down.

"I don't need any more people today," she murmured. "Let's go to the loft, if you don't mind."

"I never mind that at all."

When they walked in, Nick felt good, as he always did; the little Scottie seemed as glad to see him as he was to see Amy. While she went to the bedroom to put her things away Nick played a game of fetch with the dog, feeling his knots loosen.

She came back, looking sad and drained. He walked to her and held her, aware of how fragile her body felt, how small, inhaling the good flowery scent of her skin and hair. "I love you," he said, and he put all his heart into the saying.

"I love you, too." The way she answered chilled him; it wasn't like the way she'd said it before.

"Come on." He made his voice soft, walking her to the couch. "You're wrung out. Relax."

He pulled her head onto his shoulder and stroked her silky hair. "It's been quite a day. But tomorrow's another one." They were silent for a long few minutes.

"There's something I want to talk to you about," he began. "A—I won't say 'proposition.' That sounds too much like the office." Usually she responded to his humor but this time she didn't, only giving him another of those crooked little smiles.

" 'And what is that, Nick?' " he asked, teasing her by raising his voice, making it high in imitation of a woman's. In his own voice, he answered, "A proposal, madam."

And while she looked on, he moved a little away from her, reaching into his jacket pocket, taking out the box with the ring in it and handing it to her.

She opened it and stared at the ring. It had taken him a month, and Chandler's help, to find it. Chandler had finally come up with it from a Sotheby catalogue of Victorian jewelry in New York; it really was something, even to Nick's uneducated eye. Moonstones, her birthstone, and gray diamonds—he hadn't known that color of diamond existed—shaped almost like a half-moon, which Rhoda Silver told him was a "symbol" of Cancer.

Amy just kept staring. Without looking up, she murmured, "There's never been anything so beautiful."

He reached out and touched her face. "There's never been anything so beautiful as *you,* Amy. It had to match. Will you let me put it on . . . on the right finger?"

She looked up at him then, and her eyes were full of love, it seemed to him. But that other thing, too, that puzzling expression he couldn't fathom. An indecisiveness.

"Amy, you have to know I want to marry you, more than anything in the world," he said, bewildered. "It's the only logical conclusion, when people feel the way we do about each other. Isn't it?"

Amy nodded slowly. "Yes. It is. But what kind of wife would I be, Nick? You're in the public eye, all the time. Can you be married to a woman who's some kind of a . . . *joke?*"

He couldn't believe what he was hearing. "Damn the public eye. It's your eye, and mine, that matter. It's how we look at things that counts.

How we look at each other. And from where I sit, lady, you look perfect."

It hurt him that she still hadn't made a move to put on the ring. A horrible suspicion struck him. Could she still be carrying a torch for Pretty-Boy Windom?

"Maybe it's too soon, Nick. Maybe we should . . . go on as we are, for a little while longer. Until all this other mess blows over."

"I don't want to go on as we are, Amy. That's one reason I'm asking you to marry me. As little as I care what anybody says about me, I do care what's said about you. I couldn't take it when that idiot talked to you like a—mistress. He wouldn't dare try it if you were my wife." If he could only make her see, if he could only stop being afraid that she didn't love him, after all.

"I love you for wanting to protect me, Nick. But that's not a reason to get married."

"Of course it isn't!" She was making him crazy. "It's only one of the ten thousand or so reasons I want us to."

Now he was getting a little impatient with her continuing hesitation. And all of a sudden, the whole day piled up on him, like a demolished building: rage at himself for screwing up her day, rage at that damned reporter for dredging up the past again, and his own gnawing jealousy and uncertainty, the feelings that kept on plaguing him.

But his anger was aimed at the wrong target. Before he could stop himself, he blurted out, "You know what I think? I think you're still in love with Windom."

She got very red in the face and looked stunned. Her lips parted, then shut. Finally she said, "You know that's not true, Nick. How could you even say such a thing?"

That hesitation, he thought, had been a fraction too long. "Because it's what I believe. If you love me, you'd say yes. It's either one way or the other."

"It's not just 'one way or the other,' Nick. Not in this case. All I was saying was . . . I think we should wait a little while."

"In other words, no."

She stared at him, shaking her head, as if she didn't even know him anymore. But she said, "I didn't say that. But now I *know* we should wait."

It was a gentle kiss-off, if he'd ever heard one. Nick couldn't stand to hear any more. He walked blindly out of the loft and shut the door.

Amy sat there, staring after him. She couldn't take it in; it was too horrible.

Then she got up and ran to the door, the ring box still in her hand, calling out his name.

But when she opened the door, he was gone. After a second she walked slowly back into the apartment. She put the ring box down on a table, and stood there, looking at it sadly, wishing that she had used the right words to make him understand. And wishing he were not so agonizingly uncertain—about himself and her.

She opened the box and looked at the ring: the moonstones glimmered like the mists of dreams;

like illuminated water, or cold, pale fire. The diamonds with their gray cast were small dark stars.

Dark stars. Like the ones that seemed to follow her.

But that was absurd! Her whole life had been one of defiant effort, a life designed to overcome any "unkind fate." She'd never wasted much time feeling futile, and she wasn't going to now even if she had been a perfect drag today.

She admitted to herself that he had been very sexy, very exciting, when he hit that awful reporter. And she was disgusted with herself for being so silly all during that fabulous lunch. Even with the lunch, Nick had taken huge pains to please her.

And what if he was uncertain? What man wouldn't be, with a marital history like his? In love with a hypersensitive woman who balked and quivered at the sight of an engagement ring; acted as if some idiotic scandal sheet was the "public." If Nick was not certain of her yet, it was her job to make him so. Make him come to his senses.

Decisively she slipped the ring from its box and put it on the third finger of her left hand. In fit, proportion, and design, it was perfect. Just like everything Nick had done for her.

Just like Nick himself, stubbornness, jealousy, and all.

And she was going to call him this very minute.

Esther would be gone from the office by now. It was already nearly six o'clock. The regular number didn't answer, neither did his private phone. She got no answer at the condo, either, or at the cabin.

But there was one other place: she dialed the Tower apartment.

Rod Wales picked up the phone as the last ring died. Might have been Nick. Rod debated whether to call him or let it go till tomorrow. He hadn't seemed that fired up over the Windom deal lately and from the looks of him at lunch he might not welcome an interruption.

Rod smiled to himself. He could understand that because he was beginning to think of Rhoda as a very special lady. Rod gathered in his thoughts and got back to the report on the Japanese proposition.

He heard a footstep, the faint jingle of the Dobies' harness and looked up surprised to see Nick enter, his face as threatening as a tornado sky.

"Greetings," Rod said. "I was just wondering whether I should call you." Ace and Deuce came over to Rod and he petted them. Nick threw himself down in one of the chairs, lit a cigarette and took a vicious draw. Something was eating at him, for sure.

"What about? If it's Tokyo, that can wait." Yes, something *was* up, Rod decided. Nick was rarely this snappish.

"It's Pierrepont." That got Nick's attention. Roger Pierrepont, bosom buddy of the Windoms, owned the land adjacent to the Windoms' and had been as reluctant as they to sell to Nick. "Seems the Kaufman Group's deal went sour. I just found out a half hour ago."

133

"Well, well." Nick almost smiled. "From Bernie?" He was their slickest industrial spy.

Rod grinned. "None other. And when you think of those easements . . ."

With the easements allowed to owners of semipublic projects, Nick could make the Windoms squirm; demand rights-of-way, lay paths on their adjacent property, even blackmail them into selling Windom land to Ransom's, too.

"I *am* thinking. Where's Pierrepont now?"

"In the Caribbean. He'll be back in a few days."

"Get me on a plane tonight, Rod," Nick commanded.

"Hey, I thought there was an engagement party coming up," Rod protested. But he knew he'd put his foot in it: Nick stiffened up.

"Get me on a plane," he repeated and stalked off to the bedroom to pack.

Something damned funny was going on, Rod reflected as he dialed the airline. Nick hadn't even asked him the exact location. Anyway, why the hell couldn't he just call Pierrepont, or cable? Something must be up with Amy. Nick always ran like this when he was in a lousy mood.

Nick came back, suited up, with a bag in his hand. Rod handed him the data on his flight. "Thanks. See you in a couple of days. If the guys are too much, call Kim."

He turned on his heel and walked out.

Distracted from his work, Rod switched on the TV news. There it was—the blow-by-blow mini-movie on the afternoon's disaster.

"Nicholas—'Tough-Guy'—Ransom," the

134

woman reporter burbled, "head of the titanic Ransom Organization, raised his low profile this afternoon at the opening of the Ransom Towers in company with runaway sculptor Amy Hill, the girlfriend awarded a commission for . . ."

Rod couldn't stand to hear any more. Just before he switched the TV off, he saw a horrendous shot of Nick belting the reporter; Amy, staring with half-open lips, looking doll-like and silly, not like herself at all.

Rod hoped she wasn't looking at this right now. Maybe he ought to call her.

Better not, though. Something was wrong between those two and it was no time for a third party to interfere.

CHAPTER EIGHT

Amy rubbed her clay-stained hands on her black jumpsuit, and stood back to survey the powerful head. She'd gotten it, gotten it all, she exulted—the proud set of the head on the strong neck; the vital, springing hair and penetrating eyes. The mobile, tilted mouth and that ever-so-slight, tough and seductive slant to the nose.

She scooted down on her haunches, still gazing with delight, and took a beat-up pack of cigarettes and lighter from one of the deep pockets. She lit up, inhaling with satisfaction, thinking, *Only four days ago I believed I could never work again.*

She got up and, giving the head one more slow survey from all around, decided it was truly finished. Ready for casting. She'd have to take her time choosing the finish; think carefully about which finish would most perfectly express his essence.

Amy stretched. A long, hot bath would relieve her aching muscles. She'd been on another of those fanatic marathons. This work had gone even faster, and better, than the work she'd done for the project. Because it might be all she'd have of him.

With that thought, she felt a renewal of the awful ache that had assailed her, off and on, ever since that night. But a little later, as she relaxed in the hot water frothing with carnation-scented bubbles, some of the ache lessened in sheer physical relief.

Four days, she reflected, weren't that much in the cosmic scheme of things, but now they felt like forever. For a woman used to seeing a man every day and night, sometimes being phoned two or three times in a day, the four days stretched into eternity.

When he had walked out that night, she'd been too paralyzed with shock at first to cry. But that came, in full measure, later, especially after she'd seen that horrible newscast.

The next morning had been worse. She had to face going to the project again that afternoon, to supervise the placement of the statues. She was convinced she'd be unable to handle it, if that awful photographer showed up again. But he hadn't, thank heavens. She'd wondered if Nick had been, somehow, behind that, and just thinking of Nick hurt.

Still, the placement of the statues lifted her spirits. Whatever else happened, she still had that—her work, her gift which was her salvation. Not many people had that blessing, that receptacle for passionate emotion.

On the way back to the loft, she resolved not to watch any more TV news for a few days or even read newspapers, aside from the art news. Langella called her that afternoon to congratulate her on her reviews and that, too, helped a little.

Then she'd been visited by the wonderful inspiration: she knew exactly what would save her. Beginning a new piece.

And she'd known exactly what that piece would be.

It was hard to believe that she'd perfected it in these few days, yet when she calculated the hours she'd put in, she shouldn't have been surprised. Besides her feverish preoccupation with the work itself, she'd been bent on making herself so tired that she could just fall into bed and go to sleep.

She got into an orange top and matching pants to boost her flagging morale: the evening "antsies" were coming on. With no work at the moment and no plans, melancholy threatened.

Wandering aimlessly from room to room, she ended up in the studio again and stared at the clay head of Nick Ransom. It was so exactly like him that the mouth seemed ready to speak.

A sob escaped her; she leaned against the frame of the door, her whole body one big ache.

She'd never, in a million years, expected four days and nights to pass without a sign of him. It was incredible for a man as clear-thinking as he was to be so wrong about her, so sad that he could believe she loved Jeff Windom and never know the depth of her love for him.

The conclusion left her cold with fear. She couldn't face it. And she couldn't deal with her own foolish doubts of that day—he wasn't the only one who was uncertain. She herself hadn't had the words to make him understand, the courage to fight *his* doubt. Maybe she wasn't as strong as she'd thought.

But this was futile. If she kept thinking like this, she'd go mad. She went to get some fruit and candy together for the children. The Halloween treats would be a good distraction.

The bell rang again. Amy picked up another little bag of candy and minuscule gauze bags, each containing two quarters, and went to answer.

Peeping through the peephole, she saw only wall and smiled. Kids again, too small to be seen. Someone called out, "Trick or treat," and she hesitated. It sounded like a man's voice, disguised.

Nick's voice.

No, she must be going nutty from all this, she decided. And there was so much activity in the building tonight—a party on the floor above, children running up and down—that she wasn't nervous about opening the door. At worst it could be a plastered adult playing a joke.

When she opened the door and looked down, she was flabbergasted.

Ace and Deuce stood there, at attention. On Ace's head was a tiny black paper witch's hat; on Deuce's, an orange one. On ribbons around their necks small velvet sacks were suspended. And there were messages, she noticed as hysteria and unbelieving joy began bubbling in her: on Ace's black hat, in glittery letters, was the word FORGIVE and on Deuce's, ME?

Amy began to giggle, calling out, "Where are

you? Come out, come out, wherever you are!"
Half-sobbing, half-laughing, like an utter lunatic.

Mischief, who came to the door with Amy every time the bell rang, was agog. He started a shrill, excited barking; the stately Dobies stayed right where they were. Amy caressed them.

Smiling, Nick Ransom walked toward her from around a corner down the hall: he was dressed like a cat burglar, in a black sweater, trousers and jacket, and strode toward her soundlessly in his black, rubber-soled French "burglar's" shoes.

She was so overwhelmed she couldn't say a word.

"May we come in?" he asked her softly. "Please?"

Amy stood aside, her tears welling, and held the front door wide.

When he was holding her, Nick murmured, "Please let me tell you everything that happened, Amy. My beloved."

"Not yet. Not now. Talk can wait."

He looked at her with eyes as bright as molten silver: smiling from ear to ear, he divested the Dobies of their costumes and followed Amy to the soft-lit room beyond.

His circling arms, her seeking hands, their kisses said it all. Their swift and tacit motions told each other that they must not be apart, not one minute longer; his pleading eyes were saying that this was the beginning of forever.

At last he spoke. "From this night forward, Amy."

"From this night forward," she echoed. "Yes, oh, yes." He held her so tightly she could feel the rapid thud of his excited heart, and she murmured against him, "I couldn't live another four days like the past four, Nick. Ever."

"Neither could I."

Then they were joyfully baring their eager bodies, one to the other, and they were closer than ever, close and free and warm, caressing one another wildly, moving to the ultimate nearness with such intensity, a happiness so overpowering and profound, she almost feared her too-full heart would explode. Closer and closer they moved, in sharing and delight, until the one great, glorious moment of the burning peak; their simultaneous cry.

Drifting slowly into peace, with shuddery, short breath, they came back to themselves, fulfilled, lingering in blissful silence.

"It's too good to be true," he whispered. "Much too good to be true. Amy, you can forgive me, can't you? I'm so sorry. So sorry." He gathered her to him again.

She spoke against his hair-roughened chest, darting the tip of her tongue against his skin. She felt a ripple run along his sensitized nerves, and he made a low, moaning sound of sheer content. "I *have* forgiven you, Nick. Couldn't you tell?" she teased him.

"Stop that." Tenderly he gave her a mocking spank on her bottom, light as a feather, and she giggled.

"I've almost forgiven myself," she added softly.

"What do you mean? There's nothing for you to forgive yourself for. I was the fool, Amy. I was the juvenile rushing out into the night."

"Don't think of it. It's over." She kissed his shoulder.

"Not until we've got it straight, honey. Not until you know everything, including how I've straightened myself out. At last. I was a little crazy, thinking you were still in love with that other guy. I realize now how stupid that was. No woman has ever shown me such love as you have, Amy. Not in my whole life."

She raised her body and took his face in her hands, kissing him deeply. He gave another long, contented sigh, stroking her gloriously naked body.

She reached over him to get them cigarettes from the bed-side shelf, lighting two in her mouth, handing one to him.

"Hey, wait a minute, *I'm* supposed to be Paul Henreid," he kidded her, but the warm light in his eyes and his smiling mouth were solemn and tender.

Leaning back against him again, Amy listened as he told her the story of the four empty days. "I'd better begin at the beginning. It's something to do with . . . Boston."

He must have felt her stiffen slightly, because he squeezed her, saying quickly, "No. Not anything to do with you. Something to do with me. I don't want you to think that you do have anything to do with it, that you're part of the . . . package."

"I don't understand."

142

"You will, honey. I'm getting ahead of myself."
So he started back at the very beginning, with
what had happened to his family, when they'd
been evicted from the Windoms' own property.
She marveled at how strange it was—his world
and hers had met, after so many years; their paths
had crossed as if it had been fated.

He told her about the long years' obsession with
buying that Windom land and building a housing
development on it so beautiful and perfect, housing
so many people, that it would be a kind of kick in
the shin to the Windoms and their kind.

When he got to the part about Roger Pierrepont, she asked him eagerly, "What happened? Is
Pierrepont going to sell?"

He grinned triumphantly. "He's already sold,
honey. To me." And he explained the rest of the
ins and outs of the transaction. "As I said," he
concluded softly, "I'd hate it if you thought that
. . . getting you, *and* that tract, was a way of getting back at Jeff Windom. Although I've got to be
honest; that did enter in."

"Why shouldn't it? That's perfectly natural."

He held her close again. "You're wonderful."
After a minute he said, "You've got to be wondering how I could go for four whole days without a
word."

"I just thought it was . . . over."

"Oh, my God." His big hand caressed her hair.
"That could never happen. I was in the middle of a
small war—with myself."

She was silent, listening intently.

"First, of course, there was Project Pierrepont.

143

That took care of two days. I'd gone right back to being the old Nick Ransom." His tone was dry, full of self-mockery. "Becoming the business machine again, turning everything else off, aiming everything in me at that deal without thinking of anything else, hardly a second. As usual, it worked." He said that dismissively now, almost without interest.

"But at the end of the second day, the robot started turning human again. I couldn't keep the thoughts of you out anymore, and I hurt like hell. That night I did something I'd only done three times in my life—just got drunk alone in my room. When I came out of it, I spent a lot of time looking at myself. What I saw was a man who'd made the biggest mistake of his life. A man who let jealousy take over and rob him of his reason. When I finally got back to Chicago, just a few hours ago, I was downright afraid to call you." She took his hand.

"I figured if I couldn't get to you, maybe the Dobies could." He chuckled. "And I was right."

"Not entirely." She gave him a light kiss.

"That *reminds* me." He threw back the covers, jumped up and got into his trousers. She saw him hurry toward the living room. He came back carrying the two small velvet bags; black velvet, with golden drawstrings, dangling from one of his big fingers. With a flourish, he handed them to her.

"Happy Halloween."

In the first one was a glimmering pin in the shape of a pumpkin, formed of orange Mexican fire opals; in the other, a black onyx cat with a traditionally arched back, and peridot eyes.

"You are . . . too much," she said. "Just too much."

"No, I'm not. I'm just enough for you. I couldn't resist those little things. You know why?" She shook her head. "Because I never, in my whole damned life, had a holiday that was celebrated right. The only time there was anything at all was maybe Christmas, and even that was pretty . . . sparse."

"Now that you mention it," she said soberly, "my holidays wouldn't set the world on fire, either."

"From this night on, then, you're going to get something like this on every single one, including Groundhog Day and French Bastille Day."

She didn't know whether she was laughing or crying, but she grabbed him again and kissed him thoroughly.

"Speaking of holidays," she said with abrupt impulsiveness, "how do you feel about a party? A little one—with Rod and Rhoda, maybe."

"I like it. Because I figure we'll have something to tell them. Won't we?" He gave her a meaningful, inquiring look.

"Yes, Nick. We will."

"Oh, Amy."

When she got her breath back, she said, "I'd better get dressed. Why don't you call them?"

"You've got it." She heard him making those two calls, and then several others while she was getting herself together. With special delight, she put on her orange ensemble again, pinned on the cat and pumpkin, one above the other, on the plain scoop neck of her big tunic, and went into the living room to join him.

"I've ordered a few things," he said casually. "Some Halloween stuff and some food and a little champagne." He saw the pins, and then sighted the ring on her left hand. "Amy, you're wearing it! You mean you wore it all this time?"

She nodded. "I just . . . had to."

He hugged her.

"Look, Nick the Greek," she kidded him, "or should I say Diamond Jim . . . I've got a present for you, too. It's not quite finished, but you can see how it's going to be."

His eyes flared. "For me? Where?"

"In the studio." She led him there.

When he saw the portrait head of himself, he was speechless. He just kept looking at it and she'd never seen such happiness and such surprise on his face.

"Dearly beloved . . ."

With the minister's opening words, Amy looked up at Nick. His light-gray eyes glittered in the flames of rose-colored candles in their heavy gilded candelabra; all about them was the heavenly smell of bright-pink roses.

He had never looked quite so wonderful to her: his pearl-gray suit and discreetly textured tie of darker gray blackened his hair even more and pointed up his tanned skin and startling eyes.

She herself had made a sentimental choice of clothes for the ceremony—a three-piece, bright rose suit of tissue-weight wool, draped as softly as

146

jersey, the exact color of the suit she'd worn that day on the plane. Her shoulder-length hair had just a hint of a wave; she wore a draped turban to match the suit. And her only ornament aside from the engagement ring was a wonderful antique brooch of platinum and rose diamonds that had been Nick's wedding present.

She stood beside Nick, enchanted, in the small, hushed, jewellike chapel. Then the minister was smiling, saying, "You may kiss the bride."

And there was the exuberant sound of Mendelssohn, and they were leading the small wedding party out of the chapel into the brisk sunset of early November.

Rhoda, looking beautiful in her lilac-colored clothes, was draping Amy's long silver-blue mink, another wedding gift of Nick's, over her shoulders, taking her flowers, handing her her gloves and bag.

Accepting their congratulations, she thought how splendid they all looked, and were—Rod, in a darker gray suit; Kim in charcoal, and his girlfriend, with her dark almond eyes and sleek black hair, wearing a dress so light a gray it looked silver, emphasizing the rosy gold of her Oriental skin.

They were, as Nick suggested, keeping a low profile, to escape media attention. The announcement wouldn't be sent to the newspapers until tomorrow. Nick had even contrived, by some mysterious means, to get their marriage license without their even having to visit the license bureau. Amy had filled out her part of the application at home.

"You've got yourself a winner." Sam Langella

grabbed Amy and kissed her, turning her over to his pretty blond wife, Marta, who had chosen a wonderful shade of blue that complemented the ceremony's theme.

In line with their plan of secrecy, the eight of them split up into two limousines and drove to a sequestered restaurant in the suburbs that Nick had spotted, and where Rhoda had overseen the decorations.

The whole big private room, with its glimmering crystal chandelier and multitude of mirrors, gave back again and again the panoramic images of dozens of bright pink roses, the color of Amy's clothes . . . and the rosy world of Nick Ransom's creation.

When Nick asked Amy where she wanted to honeymoon, she'd surprised him by saying, "Not too far. I want to take the dogs and come back home. You've traveled enough, and so have I. Chicago's heavenly enough, with you, Nick. And we're both city people."

So they just took a few days, enjoying a leisurely drive through Lincoln Country. Then they drove back to Nick's summer cabin, where Amy said she would be really "home."

Amy felt now that she had never known what happiness was before. Looking at Nick, she saw that it was the same for him. For the first time, all the uncertainty was gone from his eyes: there was confidence and strength, shining from him, apparent in every intonation of his voice, in every single gesture.

* * *

Their return to the city was as joyous as their escape; whatever comment had been made in the media on their marriage, they had happily missed and intended to ignore.

Nick went back to work with zest, and Amy plunged into her new dual role with excitement. Within a few days she'd been offered several new commissions, deciding to turn down two, because there was too much else she would have to handle. She ridiculed Nick when he said, "Leave the house stuff to the staff."

He had no idea of how much was involved. Besides, as she told him sincerely, she'd been a solitary artist all her life. And now that she had a real home to make, she positively gloried in it. In a short time they moved from their temporary headquarters in the condo to a vastly larger one. Amy needed studio space, for one thing, and was using her loft at present for work during the day.

There were improvements to be made in the Tower apartment, a hundred small details which she delighted in handling. Her private deadline was Christmas, when she planned a wonderful holiday party for a large circle of friends. Thanksgiving had to be a restaurant affair, for the two of them and Rod and Rhoda. Nick had no relatives nearer than the West Coast and Southwest; Kim and his girl were visiting her people in New York and the Langellas were giving an open house of their own. Reminding Amy of his holiday promise, Nick gave her a marvelous golden cornucopia of jeweled fruits—peridots, amethysts, honey topaz and blood-red garnets, which she displayed on the neckline of a bright-gold velvet dress.

When the four met in the restaurant's foyer, Rhoda embraced Amy. "You look wonderful."

"You sure do." Rod's dark eyes admired her. "Where's my greeting?"

"Right here." Amy kissed him on the cheek.

Nick's smile disappeared; Amy saw his face stiffen. She wondered what was bothering him, continued to wonder during the early part of the lavish meal.

Then, when Rod took Rhoda to another table, to introduce her to some friends of his, Amy took Nick's hand. "Darling, something's bothering you."

"What could be bothering me? We're here together with our friends." He emphasized the last word.

"Would you have preferred just us?" she prodded. He looked so tense, and far from happy.

"I'm ashamed to tell you what's bothering me."

"Please."

"The truth is," he said, looking into her eyes, "I can't stand to see another man touch you."

"Oh, *Nick.*" She stroked his hand. That had been it, then—that meaningless, friendly kiss on Rod Wales's cheek. She could hardly believe it. But she assured him softly, "Darling, I kissed Rod the way I would . . . Rhoda, for heaven's sake. Or a brother."

He still looked unhappy. Trying to tease him out of his mood, she added, "He's in love with Rhoda, remember? That's pretty obvious. Anyway, I'm not irresistible to the entire world, the way I am to you."

"The hell you're not." But he was smiling now. He sobered. "I know it's a little crazy, honey. But I hated it when you did that."

"Well, I just won't do it anymore, then. All right?"

He nodded. "I love you so much, Amy. You're one in a million. You're not . . . angry at me, are you?"

"Never."

Everything was lovely after that, and she thought, as she watched him loosen up and begin to have a wonderful time, that his quirk was just part of him, something she'd learn to live with.

It was little enough to cope with in a man she loved so deeply, a man who worshiped her and couldn't ever seem to do enough.

Christmas was the most fairylike holiday of them all. She erected a fifteen-foot tree, the biggest one she'd ever seen in a house, decorating it with hundreds of small shining globes which, miraculously, the well-behaved dogs left alone. The tree was decorated all in one day, so that Nick could be surprised. She would never forget that one wistful comment of his about his childhood holidays, so she was determined to make this the one of his dreams. In his usual freehanded way, he'd told her to "go wild" with presents, which she'd never been able to do. So she did, not only for the pleasure of it, but also because she realized that he was one of those people to whom giving was a positive need.

151

To keep him from giving was like trying to tell a fruit tree not to bear fruit.

To add to their gaiety, Rod and Rhoda announced they were going to be married on December thirtieth, "right under the wire" for New Year's Eve. Nick said they should combine a wedding and Christmas present into something really "sensational." Nick underwrote the honeymoon, in its entirety, and Amy bought Rhoda a fabulous pair of aquamarine and diamond earrings.

When Nick came home on Christmas Eve and walked into the high-ceilinged living room and caught sight of the tree, Amy knew that nothing else she could give him would mean as much. It was as if all he had ever desired were here, in this room with her, and the animals; all that had been grinding and dreary, shabby and worn in his bitter childhood, was canceled out. But far more significant and profound, the loneliness, the longing of their adult lives were at an end. Their minds were married, too.

On a rain-misted afternoon the next April, Amy's favorite kind of weather, she added the last sure touch to a figure of exuberant children, thinking how different it was from the poignant girl with the ball that she had sculpted for the housing project.

This piece had been commissioned for the elaborate fountain on an estate in suburban Oak Park, "Frank Lloyd Wright country," and Amy had greatly enjoyed the doing of it. Now all that re-

152

mained was the casting and the all-important patina.

The child-figures, which would ultimately be placed in the center of the splashing fountain, looked utterly carefree, their **hands** and arms raised in splashing gestures; they symbolized the change in Amy herself, no more like her earlier figures than Amy Hill Ransom was like Amy Hill.

The months of marriage to Nick Ransom had changed her a great deal, bringing to her a sense of security she had never believed she'd have. She had a flashback to her insight on that happy Christmas Eve, when Nick's eyes, observing the big tree, had been so eloquent.

Langella had seen it, too. He told her she'd brought new life and meaning to the traditional. The realism that was her special gift had acquired a suggestion of the mystery that glimmered beyond the concrete, the palpable object. Langella urged her to prepare for another and larger exhibition. Soon she would, now that all the practical arrangements of her life with Nick were out of the way.

Thinking of Christmas Eve put her in the mood to reminisce; she tidied herself up a bit and wandered into the little living room outside her studio, a cozy place she'd set up for herself and Nick to relax in, separate from the splendor of the big one where they entertained.

Here the tweedy sofa and the leather chairs could cope with her clay-dabbled gear, and there was a homey, very doggy aroma about it. Nick said it was his favorite room. They kept their monumental collection of snapshots here, and Amy took one of the albums from a shelf as Mischief settled onto his favorite leather hassock.

She turned the pages, glancing through the snapshots of the last three happy months, amazed how fast they'd gone: one of herself and Nick and Rod and Rhoda, taken on Christmas evening after the other guests had gone; one from New Year's Eve, when they had entertained the newlyweds at a quiet party at home, the image pulsating with gaiety and color—Amy in a hot-pink evening gown, wearing her New Year's pin, a small, stylized champagne glass of crystal and diamonds; Rhoda starry-eyed in a blue dress the color of her eyes.

Valentine's Day, with its garnet heart; Easter, bringing pearl eggs.

They had given so much to each other. She had softened some of his stony hardness while he had bolstered her with his strength, and educated her in the bewildering ways of the "real world" so strange to an artist who had always occupied her own.

Amy had discovered that being a "business wife" on occasion was no hardship at all; in fact, she enjoyed it. There were certain things, she had always felt, a wife must do. Nick was touchingly grateful to her for it, proud to display his "beautiful, gifted" wife. But he still kept such occasions to a minimum, preferring, as she did, small gatherings or occasions for two.

Their way of life had become so familiar she sometimes forgot that there had ever been another way. Nothing rocked their magic boat. The media were leaving them in peace.

The only minor problem—and measured against the rest, it was minor—was an occasional flash of Nick's old jealousy. Nevertheless, after the incident on Thanksgiving, there had been nothing major. Amy was very careful now to be aloof from other men. It was her nature to be casual and friendly, so there were times when it made her uncomfortable to have to watch every word and gesture. Still, the effort had been worth it. Nick had never looked so happy or secure as he did now.

Putting the album back, Amy petted Mischief. It was time to get in some "human clothes," as she styled them, before Nick got home. She showered and changed into a new yellow lounge dress. While she was making up she began to wonder about the Windom project. Nick had been very cagey about it since last winter, but she had a feeling it would surface again soon.

She went down the curving stairs and made some cocktails to welcome him. The huge living room with its colorful spring touches looked very inviting. The Dobies were lying near the front door, knowing that Nick would be there shortly, that after cocktails he'd take them for their run.

Hearing his key in the door, she decided to give him a special welcome. She poured a drink and went to meet him with it. As always, his eyes lit up when she opened the door. His raincoat was sopping, the collar turned up rakishly around his neat ears, his bare head damp.

"Well, what's all this?" He took the glass from her, embracing her with his other arm. "You make me feel like the king of the world."

He took a swallow of the drink and set it on a console table. Shedding his coat he took his cocktail to the couch and sat down with her, petting Mischief and the Dobies, competing for his attention.

"Okay. Give me a *chance,* dogs." They backed off politely. He seemed a bit pressed, Amy thought. He definitely had something on his mind.

"How did it go today?" she asked casually.

He took another swallow of his drink. "There's a lot happening. I'm afraid I might have to go to Boston."

Hypersensitively she registered the "I," but she said in a level voice, "Oh?" She sensed his keen glance on her profile.

"Yes. Rumor has it that the Windoms are about to cave in. I've got to get up there before they change their minds."

"I see." She heard the slight chill in her voice.

"Honey, what's the matter?"

"Oh . . . well, you did it twice." He looked puzzled. "Said *'I.'* "

"Amy." He hugged her to him. "I took it for granted you're going. Don't you know that?" He kissed the top of her head, squeezing her shoulder. "We'll take the company plane, so we can haul the dogs along and stay in an apartment I have there. While I'm wheeling and dealing, you can do the museums and stores. I'd like you to see the site with me too, since you *are* going to be doing the artwork."

In spite of herself, Amy had a totally contrary reaction. First she'd been miffed because she

156

thought he was going alone; now she was uncertain. It wasn't quite a year since she'd made her sensational exit from the Windoms' Boston.

"Nick, do you think . . ." She stopped.

"Think what?"

"That it's a good idea for me to do the sculpture? I mean, after what happened. My sculpture on Windom land. It's . . ." She broke off. He looked irritated. She wished she hadn't said that.

"First of all," he answered a bit sharply, "it won't be Windom land. It'll be Ransom land. Anyway, all that's history."

He looked at her. "Isn't it?" For the first time in months, she glimpsed the ghost of his old jealousy.

"Of course it is." She cupped his face in her hands and kissed him. But his lips were cool and he didn't relax.

He drew away from her. "I wish I could be sure, Amy."

Hot anger washed over her. "I don't see why you can't be. Don't do this to me, Nick. I can't stand not being trusted. It hurts. It's . . . exasperating. What do I have to *do* to make you believe me? I can't do any more than I have already."

She could still see that faint shadow in his light-gray eyes. "I guess you can't." He got up abruptly. "I'm going to take the dogs out."

He left without kissing her. Leaning against the closed door, she thought, *I've got to make this right. Nothing in the world is going to come between us. Not even Nick himself.*

His jealousy was the only real enemy they had.

CHAPTER NINE

When she heard his key, she was waiting. She threw her arms around him, kissed his face and neck. "Let's don't fight. Please. I love you so much."

"Oh, Amy." He let go of the dogs' leashes, pulled her closer to him. "I'm sorry. I love you *too* much."

"Let's forget it."

"It's forgotten."

Yet she felt it wasn't. Even when she told him she'd finished the latest piece, asking, "How's that for timing?" his enthusiasm sounded forced.

And when they went into the glass-walled dining room, with its sweeping twilight view of the shore, he hardly seemed to see what pains she'd taken. He made no comment on the yellow tulips and the yellow linen cloth chosen to counteract the gray weather he disliked.

"I don't know what you'll think of the place in Boston," he remarked, taking absent bites of food. Then he veered off, "It looks more and more like old man Windom's going to come around. When Pierrepont sold it knocked Windom off his perch

. . . the idea of 'peasants' having access to his precious turf will be the deciding factor, I think." Nick seemed to be talking *at* her.

"Why has he held on and held on?"

"Sheer stubbornness. The land's been in the family for a couple of hundred years. All he had on it before was tenements—including the one we lived in." Nick gave her his ironic smile.

She listened as he went on, forcing interest, wishing she could take that look out of his eyes; that they could talk *to* each other again. He was preoccupied all the rest of the evening and that night they did not make love.

The tense mood persisted throughout their flight and their arrival in Boston. Nick had that expression she had come to know so well—that absent, plotting look that preceded a coup.

That night they dined in the famous Harper House, still the bastion of great cuisine. Amy was beginning to feel more relaxed, because Nick was, too.

He complimented her on her sherry-colored dress; the color was a pleasant note against the walnut-paneled walls, the brown and beige decor.

It was difficult even to remember the problems of the night before.

Then she saw a tall, blond man come in the dining room with an elegant blond woman in black.

It was Jeff Windom.

Nick hadn't seen him yet; his back was to the door, but Jeff had seen Amy. While he was seating his companion, he stared at her across the room.

To her dismay, Amy saw him bend to the elegant blond, say something to her, and walk toward Nick's and Amy's table.

"Amy?" Jeff murmured, when he was standing beside them. He sounded uncertain. "It *is* you. I didn't recognize you at first." She wasn't surprised; she was hardly the old Amy.

Nick was getting to his feet. His face was carefully bland, but Amy had a sinking sensation.

"Hello, Jeff." She was gratified that her voice was so steady. "I'd like you to meet my husband, Nick Ransom. Jeff Windom." She thought, *Nick makes him look like a boy*.

There was the slightest flicker in Nick's pale eyes; they had a hard cast when he shook hands.

"Congratulations," Jeff said, sounding sincere. Grotesquely so, Amy reflected, considering the circumstances.

"Thanks." Nick was still facing Jeff in the manner of a man measuring an opponent. "Will you join us?" he asked stiffly.

"No. No, thank you," Jeff said quickly. "My date is waiting for me. Er, nice to meet you, Mr. Ransom. Good to see you both."

Nick sat down again and glanced at Amy; she felt, uneasily, that the glance did not quite meet hers. She reached across the table and put her hand on top of his.

"Well, well. The son and heir in living color. That picture didn't do him justice. You never mentioned that." Nick's eyes were accusing. She felt a stirring of resentment.

"Of course I didn't. Because it didn't matter."

160

"*Didn't* matter?" It distressed her that he had picked up on her every word like that.

"Doesn't matter, darling. Not now or ever." It was an effort to keep her answer even and gentle, when she felt a little like snapping at him.

"Are you sure, Amy?" Nick was studying her. "Is the old flame really out?"

"How can you ask me that, Nick . . . after all we've been to each other?" This time she tried to put all her love, all the reassurance she could muster, into her question. "There's nothing left for him at all, Nick. There hasn't been since the night of that concert. Remember?" He smiled at that. Then, as it turned out, she put her foot in it.

"He was only being polite. And generous, really, after what I pulled," she added.

Nick's straight black brows shot up. " 'Generous'? I don't think that's the word. 'Interested' would be my guess, Amy."

"Oh, *Nick.*" She stroked the hard fingers under hers, but they didn't respond much. "I love you. I love you with all of me. Please . . . believe me."

"I do, Amy. I'm a fool. I'm sorry." His wide smile heartened her.

Eager to change the subject, even if it was an equally awkward one, she asked, "How did it go today? You still haven't told me. I mean, the idea of my contribution to the project," she ended wryly.

"No one mentioned that at all. So far we've been leading a charmed life with the media." They certainly had—she'd seen no reference to the notorious team of Nick and Amy Ransom on the TV news or in any scandal sheets. "Don't worry about that, honey. No one's going to bar my wife from a Ransom project."

She decided not to, nor let anything else spoil the rest of their evening. With relief she noticed that Jeff and his companion had apparently only stopped for cocktails; when she and Nick left, they were gone.

And at the evening's end she demonstrated sweetly to Nick how little he had to be jealous of. By the next morning his confidence seemed fully restored.

Then that very afternoon she saw a TV news report that chilled her: someone, somehow, had gotten hold of the information that the sculpture of Amy Hill Ransom, who had spurned the Windoms, might well be decorating former Windom land.

She could tell it was the work of the *Last Word.* Arthur Mason, that obnoxious photographer, may have decided not to charge Nick with assault or sue, but he had other ways to avenge himself. Continuing the harassment, for one.

Amy recalled an occasion at Nick's office, right before their marriage. She'd dropped in to meet Nick's secretary, Esther, for lunch and Rod Wales had come in to join the friendly gathering. He carried a sheaf of bills.

Seeing Amy and Esther, Rod looked sheepish.

"What's up?" Nick asked.

Rod had hesitated, then said, "These. I think they're out of line."

Nick glanced at the bills and chuckled. "Oh,

yeah, the camera, and Mason's jacket. Well, well." He'd seemed vastly amused. "What the hell, Rod, pay it. Cheap at the price, wouldn't you say?"

Amy recalled she couldn't help laughing, both at Esther's bewildered expression and Nick's implication that there hadn't been lawyers' fees and medical bills.

But now her smile died away. Hard to believe that the obnoxious Mason could arouse such a furor over just two men and a woman, considering all the serious things in the world.

But, she concluded sardonically, people like Jeff Windom and Nick and Amy Ransom were not entitled to privacy in the minds of people like Mason. They were perfect targets for scandal rags: the scion of the high-and-mighty Windoms; the woman who had had the temerity to reject one— "and everybody knows what those *artists* are like," Amy quoted to herself with bitter humor, and most of all, publicity-shy Nick Ransom who'd always held himself aloof from the obligatory glamour of the Beautiful People.

What a creep that Mason was, with his fat face, foolish mustache and malicious little eyes.

Annoyed, Amy snapped off the TV set. She was leashing the dogs for a run when Nick walked in.

"Hello." She hurried to grab him around the neck and give him a big kiss of welcome. "You're early."

"Late is more like it," he groaned, returning her caress a bit absently. He tossed his briefcase on a table. "You're going out. Come on, I'll go with you. We can talk. I've got some new problems."

"Oh, I'm sorry."

"Come on, guys." Nick took the Dobies' tandem leash and left Mischief's to Amy. "Ready?" He smiled at her, but she could see his tension and impatience.

"Sure."

When they were entering the nearby park, he said, "Let's sit a minute, honey." Then he continued, "I guess you saw that damned newscast."

She nodded and then she felt sudden guilt. If it weren't for her, none of this would be happening.

"It's absolutely ridiculous," he went on, "but all of a sudden, now, there's a ruckus. Old Man Windom's balking about the final sale, and somehow Washington's gotten into it. I got a call from Hugo Benson."

Benson was Nick's federal contact since Nick's public housing project depended on partial federal funding. "I see. The delay in the land sale is making them nervous. Is that it?"

"Partly."

"How does the newscast enter in?"

Nick looked irritated. "It's so damned stupid. Apparently that rotten Mason put the idea of sinecures and corruption in their heads. Got them convinced that I'm planning a kind of Taj Mahal with public money," he scoffed.

"Oh, that's outrageous."

"Damned right it is. The upshot is that I've got to fly down to Washington this afternoon, talk to Hugo and some other people, go over the specs with them again. Meanwhile Rod's flying here with one of the lawyers to take up negotiations.

There's just a chance that Windom could be in legal jeopardy by stalling like this, but I don't think so."

"I'll go with you," she offered.

"It wouldn't be worth it, Amy. At the most I'll be there overnight."

She thought dolefully, overnight wasn't "at the most" to him before. He'd always said he couldn't stand to be away from her, even for a single night. But she dismissed the idea; Nick had enough on his mind without her sulking.

"I'd better go, honey."

Back at the apartment, she packed a small bag for him, trying not to feel hurt when he insisted on going to the airport alone. She remembered their first encounter at Logan, and his claiming that's where he'd fallen in love with her. He certainly wasn't thinking about that now.

She was immediately ashamed of herself for being so childish. When she kissed him good-bye at the door, while the taxi waited, Amy clung to him. "I'll miss you."

"I'll miss you too," he answered, but he sounded impatient again, perfunctory.

Watching the cab drive off, Amy told herself not to think like an idiot. He was under extreme pressure; this enterprise was precious to him, for the best of reasons. He'd told her again and again that it was a promise he'd made to himself a long time ago, and to his parents. In fact, the project itself would be named for them.

Even if she felt at odds, without her studio and

no definite plans, she'd damned well make some and keep busy.

It was a mild, beautiful day and she'd never really explored Boston. That kind of thing had bored Jeff to distraction; it hadn't mattered to him, she recalled with a flash of ancient resentment, that it might appeal to her. Nick, with his constant attention to her wishes, was the complete opposite of Jeff.

And she'd been sulking because Nick had to go away . . . irrationally bemoaning the fact that she was his "albatross." She was thoroughly ashamed; she was one of the luckiest women alive, free to do whatever she wanted.

It might be fun to do some museums, maybe some shopping. Amy dressed in a cocoa-colored walking suit, enlivened its dark brown tunic with the cornucopia pin of light green and gold, orange and scarlet gems. It reminded her of the Horn of Plenty that was life with Nick, both in the seen and unseen treasures.

Amy knew that Boston cabdrivers were often an education in themselves since they were often Harvard students driving for extra money. She drew one of those now, to her gratification. She asked him to take her to the Museum of Fine Arts and got a minicourse in Boston's extraordinary museums. He also told her there was a concert at four that day at the Isabella Stewart Gardner Museum. He was a fine arts major, it turned out.

The driver said, "You're very knowledgeable."

She answered mildly, "In a way," and saw him

look at her in the driver's mirror. She wondered if he could possibly recognize her, feeling haunted.

But she was in much better spirits when she left the Fine Arts Museum, second only to New York's Metropolitan among the country's great museums. It would have taken a lifetime to cover all of the Fine Arts' two hundred galleries, but she'd settled for her favorites, Whistler, Sargent, and Hassam, recalling America's youth; lingered over sculpture, enchanted with the figure of a dancer whose bronze drapes seemed as liquid as chiffon, wafted by an invisible breeze.

She went from there to the Gardner. It was like walking into a Venetian palazzo of the last century. The famous Mrs. Gardner had lived in the house for nearly a quarter of that century and filled it with the stuff of dreams. Amy wandered through a lily-planted courtyard that took her breath. Steeped in beauty, she was almost able to forget the pressure and anxiety of Nick's last-minute trip without her.

Throughout the house were masterpieces in oil, exquisite antique furniture and stained-glass windows. The concert was held in the Tapestry Room; the wonderful tapestries were hung below a ceiling of massive beams and Amy stepped on a superbly tiled floor.

But she had only "almost" forgotten. The mourning brightness of the music recalled Nick again, and she missed him, disproportionately, with a positive ache in her heart.

She tiptoed out and went back to the apartment, consoled by the affectionate presence of the animals. She gave them their dinners, took them for another outing, and wondered what she was going to do with the night.

Her own meal was indifferently ordered from the chef service, half eaten. There were neither books nor television programs that appealed to her; she wondered why Nick hadn't called. She debated whether she'd go to a movie and finally decided to.

As much to lift her morale as anything, she chose an especially glamorous suit; she opted for a sheer-escape spy film which likely would have little to do with love, she judged. She was wrong. The movie was colorful and amusing, but it also had an atypical love story and that made her start to ache and worry, all over again.

The theater wasn't far from the Copley. When she came out, it was still fairly early, not yet ten. Feeling hungry after her sparse dinner, Amy went into one of the Copley's five restaurants—a lounge full of plants and stained glass where a single woman could be comfortable. She'd been there once with Jeff's mother after a shopping trip.

The agreeable lounge contrasted sharply with the male atmosphere of the adjoining barroom, featuring an oak and leather bar; the dining rooms favored by "Proper Bostonians." She had a light sandwich and a small glass of white wine. When she was leaving she heard a man's voice calling out her name in well-modulated tones. A Boston accent.

She turned and saw Jeff Windom. "Amy!" he repeated with pleasure. He was the last person on

168

earth she wanted to see, but couldn't help noticing that he looked especially splendid in faultless gray flannel and a blue cravat doubtless chosen to match his eyes. His gold hair had a Tiffany gleam.

She couldn't escape now, he was coming toward her. He had the friendliest, most human smile on his face that she had ever seen him display.

"You're ravishing," he said softly, looking at her severe black suit with its Ming yellow blouse, the small gold dragon on her lapel enameled in pulsing scarlet, yellow, and green. "You were always beautiful. Now you're magnificent."

With a tight half-smile, she murmured, "It's . . . nice to see you, Jeff. I'd better be leaving."

"Why?" he demanded. "Your husband's in Washington."

Of course. He would know that; he might also have been involved in the negotiations.

"Surely you can spare a few minutes for a drink . . . for auld lang syne."

Surely she could, Amy admitted, after what she'd done to him and his family. "All right. A few minutes. And only one."

"Wonderful." He escorted her into the massive barroom where an attentive waiter gave them a small, round table near the window. Jeff ordered and smiled at her. She thought, *There's something very different about him.*

"This is nice," he said. "I've been longing for this chance to ask for your forgiveness."

"My forgiveness!" She was flabbergasted. "Jeff, that's—"

He took her hand across the table in such an insistent grasp that she couldn't free it.

"Please, let me say it, Amy. All of it. The scandalmongers and my relatives cast you as the heavy. When all the time *I* was. *We* were."

She was astonished but kept her silence, waiting to hear how he had reached such a conclusion.

He paused while the waiter placed their cocktails before them, then let go of her hand, raising his glass. "To the truth," he said lightly. His blue eyes above the shining rim were serious, though.

She followed suit. "To the truth, then."

They sipped and Jeff went on, "Everyone was so intent on what you did to me that they never stopped to realize what we had done to you, Amy. I must admit," he raised a golden brow, "I was slightly discombobulated when the bride of the great Jeff Windom acted like a Bride of Dracula."

She flushed, but he was chuckling.

"Then when things calmed down," he continued, "and you were so conscientious in every small detail"—she assumed that was his discreet way of referring to the return of the ring, the keys, the gown—"I started to remember all the qualities in you that just enchanted me. I recalled telling you that you reminded me of a portrait in Boston."

He grinned, and that white grin still had, even now, a certain dubious charm, she confessed to herself.

"You never saw the portrait. Do you know whose it was? It was the portrait of another lady who got away, from one of my illustrious ancestors. We never even knew her name, but the family kept the painting as a curiosity. I realized how eerie that was. And my sister, of all people, let me have it."

"Your sister?" *She'd been the least receptive of them all,* Amy thought, bewildered.

"I know. She was certainly never nice to you. But she had the sense to know, from the start, we weren't right for each other; that there was no reason you *should* adapt to Windom ways. She accused me of wanting to marry you just to upset the family. And, I blush to admit it, Amy, but there was a lot of truth in that." His cheekbones actually reddened. "If I'd loved you enough, we'd have been married in Chicago. I'd have understood about your work . . . even the little dog."

"Jeff . . . when did all this *happen* to you . . . these insights, I mean?"

"When I got together again with Alexandra." He noticed her expression. "Oh, yes, my uncle heard that, too, at the church. I guess it was true all along. We're going to be married in May."

"I'm so glad, Jeff." She meant it sincerely. Now the past *was* laid to rest. She couldn't wait for Nick to find that out. If she could somehow introduce the subject, tactfully . . .

The thought of Nick reminded her of the time. She looked at her wafer-thin gold watch, exclaimed, "I really must go, Jeff. Nick might be trying to phone me."

"I think not," he said, smiling mysteriously. "He's probably on a plane right now, coming back to Boston."

"Why on earth do you say that?"

"Because I just left my father, and our lawyers, in one of the dining rooms. My father's signed the bill of sale." Jeff grinned at her. "Mostly at my urging."

Her first thought was, *How wonderful for Nick.* Her second, *Why at Jeff's urging?*

She asked him.

He laughed. "Oh, not for you or your husband, sweetheart. You know me too well. I could never masquerade as noble."

That was true enough, she thought.

"For the money, Amy. The lovely, lovely money. Money for Alexandra and me. My father's held on to that white elephant against our wishes."

She digested the information a moment in dazzled silence. Then she wondered aloud, as if she were completely alone, "I wonder if Nick knows yet?"

"Of course! His partner—Wales, is it?—called him in Washington to tell him."

Studying her thrilled face, he asked curiously, "What is it about that land, Amy, if I may be so personal? I mean, what's made Ransom so hot for that particular tract? Part of the feud with me?"

She felt her cheeks heat. "Partly. But a great deal more, too, Jeff. Much more." Deciding it would do no harm now, she told him a little of the history of Nick's parents.

"So that's it. I understand now. I really understand," Jeff murmured.

"It seems to me you've gotten *very* understanding," she teased him. "Do we owe some of that to Alexandra?"

She noticed how his eyes and whole face brightened with the mention of her name. "A lot of it, Amy. She's a remarkable woman. We've known each other all our lives, have the same points of reference."

"Like Nick and me," she said companionably.

He nodded. "Sure. Alexandra's not like the old dinosaurs, who think in terms of 'worse' and 'better.' She speaks in terms of 'different.' What was that quote in the big Civil War movie?"

" 'There can only be real happiness when like marries like,' more or less," Amy supplied. She thought of herself and Nick, the similarities in their lives.

"Won't she be wondering where you are?"

"Not on your life, my dear. I spoke to her right before I ran into you. She's so frazzled from fêtes and fittings, she said, that she was half-asleep. I'll be going right back to my lonely bed, right after I drop you off. You'll allow me to, won't you . . . after we have one more?"

"I really don't know if I should wait, Jeff," she said uneasily. What if Nick had flown back, and was at the apartment right now? "I think I'd better pass that up, and just hop into a cab myself. Ungracious as that sounds after all the nice things you told me."

"May I be ungallant, then, and just let you go on? I've had a pretty full day, and I really could use another belt or two."

"Of course," she insisted warmly. "Before I go, though, I'd like to say something to you, Jeff."

She felt so very warmly toward him now, as if

173

they were old, dear friends, and the past was so securely behind them, that she put her hand on his.

"I want to say I'm sorry, Jeff. Once and for all. I am sorry for all the embarrassment and trouble I caused you and your family. It takes two to tango, you know; I should have known better, too."

Amy leaned toward him slightly.

Jeff leaned forward, too, putting his other hand over hers. "Thanks, Amy." He squeezed her hand.

"Always my beautiful and generous girl," he murmured.

Someone else, she noticed from the corner of her eye, had heard that last sentence. She saw that a man was standing right beside them.

She looked up, a bit startled, into Nick Ransom's blazing silver eyes.

It was like being in the middle of a nightmare, because he was looking at her with the eyes of a stranger.

CHAPTER TEN

Nick had felt just like this as a kid, when he'd taken the first roundhouse from his opponent: his stomach felt sick and he was punchy with the shock. Finding Amy like this with Windom.

The odds were a million to one against it. His taxi had happened to slow in traffic right beside the Copley. He'd dismissed the cab there, walked toward the window, seen them holding hands.

Walked to their table on Windom's line, "My beautiful and generous girl." And they'd been so intent on each other they hadn't even *seen* him.

Amy was saying something about being glad to see him, but Nick could hardly hear her for the angry roaring in his head. He wanted to shout, demand why she had done this.

But he got his voice in control. *"Your* girl?"

Windom was on his feet now. He and Nick were taking each other's measure.

Nick felt Amy's light touch on his arm, heard her pleading, "Nick—" Heard her because he still wasn't looking at her; he just kept staring at Pretty Boy, there.

This time, when he glanced down at her, the

beautiful face he knew by heart was very pale, her brown eyes enormous.

"I'll put you in a cab, Amy." Nick listened to his own voice, hard and quiet and tightly controlled. He put his hand on her shoulder, with gentle pressure asking her to come with him. "I'll be right back, Windom. There are a couple of things I'd like to . . . discuss with you."

Windom, still standing, retorted, "There's something I'd like to discuss with you. I'll be waiting."

Nick could just bet there was. "Amy?"

Now she looked angry, very angry. "I'll put myself in my own cab," she said coldly, got up and walked out before he could stop her.

He started after her. Windom said sharply, "Wait a minute, Nick, before you go off half-cocked and make it worse—"

Nick wasn't thinking very straight right then but he concluded it was just as well—he felt like knocking Windom through the plate-glass window. And if he did, he didn't want Amy to see it or get caught in any flying shrapnel.

"Ransom to you, pal," he returned. His voice was as quiet as it had been before, but now he could let go with the full anger.

"Sit down, why don't you? Have a drink."

Pretty Boy's calm was getting to Nick. He leaned on the table, his face close to Windom's. "I don't know what it is with you. Maybe you've got a death wish."

"Far from it, Ransom. I'm no match for you at all, and I've got to be in shape for my wedding. I'm asking you again, please. Sit down. Let's talk."

The guy had nerve, Nick would say that for him. Then the meaning of Windom's words sank into Nick's rage-befuddled brain. *In shape for my wedding.* Sheer amazement weakened Nick's knees, and he sat down opposite Windom almost before he knew it. *"Wedding?"*

"To a lovely lady named Alexandra Hale," Windom said. Nick could hear relief in his not-quite-steady answer; the guy *hadn't* been happy about tangling with him. "A lady I've known since I was a child. Somebody who's as right for me as you and Amy are for each other. *That's* what we were talking about when you came in. I said she was beautiful and generous because she is: she was saying she was sorry for what she'd done to me and my family. After she'd told me how glad she was that I'm marrying Alexandra."

Nick was still trying to take it in. My God. And he'd been thinking . . . "But you were . . . holding each other's hands, man. What the hell was I supposed to think?"

"Not holding hands. Touching hands in friendship, Ransom. Amy was just about to leave. To go home, so she'd be sure to be there when you got back."

"What do you mean, when I got back?" Nick demanded. "How would you know that?"

"Because," Windom told him patiently, "I was in negotiations with my father and heard your partner call you in Washington to give you the news."

"You were part of the negotiations."

"Of course." Windom finally smiled, now that

things were simmering down, now that Nick was taking it all in. "My family's been trying to get rid of that land for years."

"I can't believe it," Nick said, stunned.

"Believe it, Nick."

This time his first name didn't bother Nick at all. He swore softly. "Look here, Windom. I've made one hell of a mistake."

"You surely did. Your timing was terrible. If you'd gotten here a little earlier, you could have seen how Amy looked when your name was mentioned. I've never seen a woman who's so much in love with her husband."

Nick got to his feet and held out his hand. "I'm sorry."

Jeff Windom got up, too, and shook his hand. He was grinning now. "Don't tell me. Tell Amy."

That was just what Nick was going to do . . . if it wasn't too late already.

Too impatient to wait for a cab, he started jogging toward the apartment.

Amy dabbed at her streaming eyes. Her anger had abated, almost as soon as she had reached the apartment, quickly replaced by the most profound hurt she'd ever known.

She couldn't forget the blank hardness of Nick's light-gray eyes, looking at her, through her, as if he didn't even *know* her. In all the time of their acquaintance, he'd never looked at her like that. It struck her to the very core.

Even at the beginning, at the airport, when they hadn't even known each other's names, or anything about each other, his eyes had been gentle, anxious, and concerned.

But in that nightmare instant at the Copley, those familiar eyes had looked as impenetrable as flat gray stones.

It was hard to believe after that that his love was as solid and sure as he had always claimed. That possessive, almost desperate love of his that had no trust in it at all.

How he could have so misread what he had seen —the friendly touch of her hand on Jeff's, affecting her no more than Langella's touch would have, for heaven's sake . . . or Rod's, or Kim's. It was horrible, unreal.

She sobbed, and Mischief jumped up on the couch with a worried expression, licking her face; the Dobies prowled restlessly, sensing something was very wrong.

She ached from the betrayal of his faith in her. And in himself, if it came to that.

The sound of the key in the door made her jump. The Dobies and Mischief, alerted by the sound, trotted toward the opening door.

Nick stood there, and his face was pleading. Frightened.

"Amy. Oh, Amy, you're here," he said inanely, and that very inanity, so unusual in him, touched her.

"Of course I am," she cried out in pained resentment. "You know damned well I couldn't run away and leave the dogs."

He came slowly toward her and knelt down beside her, looking at her with eyes that weren't blind and hard any longer, but naked with pain.

But he made no move to touch her, as if he had no right. "You wouldn't run away from *here*. What scared me was you'd run away from me. In your mind and your heart. For good."

She thought, *Jeff must have told him about Alexandra; told him how things really are.* And the miracle was that Nick had listened.

The look of him, and what he said, began to melt the tight, hard knot of resentment inside her. She reached out a tentative hand but didn't touch him yet. He noticed the small gesture, though, and his hopeful expression moved her.

He bowed his head. She could see he was struggling for control. Then he raised his head again, pleading with her, "Can you forgive me?"

Her first impulse was to tell him yes. But she couldn't, not yet. He'd hurt her too much, too often.

Their gazes held. She could see the love and shame in his, the awful fear that he might lose her.

"It's been so hard," she said softly. "So painful. Do you know how awful it is, to love someone so completely . . . and not be able to convince him?" He blushed, looking miserable. "I never did anything to make you mistrust me, yet you keep accusing me of nonexistent wrongs. I'm not Janet, Nick. I never was. It's horrible to be treated like her."

He nodded slowly. She'd never mentioned his wife's name before, never mentioned her at all, but now she had to. They had to open up totally with each other.

"So many times," she said, "I knew that you compared yourself unfavorably with Jeff Windom."

"Yes. I did."

"And all the time, Nick, I was delighted that you weren't Jeff. I loved you because you weren't like him. Don't you know that?"

He was getting up, speechless, looking at her with his heart in his eyes. And never, in all the time they had known each other, had she seen such pride and triumph in his eyes.

"I know now, Amy. And I know something else —I've been the biggest fool in the Western world."

He held out his hand. She took it, and he urged her gently upward, encircling her with his arms.

She was crying now, crying from sheer happiness.

Their kiss began gently, too. But then it took fire.

Nick raised his mouth from hers; his eager breath was hot against her hair. She felt her body tremble and ignite.

Aware of his strong excitement, she was conscious that her own wild needs were answering his. It had never been quite like this before between them. She felt a new stirring as his hard arms pressed her close again; knew from his very touch that he perceived her feeling. He stroked her breasts. Excitement darted all along her skin.

Gently he eased her jacket off and laid it on a chair, kneeling down before her, caressing her again; a caress that almost burned her skin below the sliding fabric.

Hardly knowing what she did, Amy leaned over and kissed his thick black hair, stroked his sinewy neck as his hold upon her tightened.

Her heart was full and pounding when he raised his head to look up at her again with those keen, triumphant eyes.

He got to his feet. Still fixing her with that magnetic stare, he scooped her up in his arms and strode into the bedroom, closing the door on their own private world.

She was breathless in his grasp, melting against the hardness of his chest and arms. She seemed to be flowing into him, around him.

He set her down, and swiftly began to undress her, kissing another part of her body each time another garment was tossed away.

He urged her to the bed and she looked at him with pleasure as he flung off his own clothes, until his own tanned, hard body was bare also. In the dim light, his massive shoulders had an awesome power; more than ever, his lean power moved her, and she felt as if it were the first time, all over again.

He knelt above her then, and she saw his dark head lower, felt the rhythmic start of the caress so poignant that at first she could barely tell it from pain; but then that strange sensation, as it always had before, became a burning point of light, a pleasure so acute she cried out in her happiness. In the complete meeting of their bodies, she found an even greater fulfillment.

Never . . . never had their love been quite so overpowering or so sweet. The light broke through her dazzled lids, the inner fires, once more ignited, spread, this time with even more tremendous force into a wheeling blaze of breaking light. She heard his outcry and it spoke to her heart.

Close in his arms she was a wanderer back at home.

In the passenger lounge of the Ransom jet, Nick looked up from the report he was studying. He glanced at Amy and his heart turned over.

They had been up talking half the night, but you couldn't tell by looking at her. She looked as bright as the sunset through the window; her eyes were big and glowing. Inspired.

She was sketching out ideas for the project sculpture. Her apple-red dress made a pleasing splash of color against the pale gray chair. Mischief was a darker gray blur on the carpet by her feet. The little jeweled jet glittered on the neckline of her dress.

Sensing his scrutiny she looked up from her sketch pad and smiled.

"It's a far cry from that first flight, isn't it?" he murmured.

"Another world." She reached over and took his hand, and his heart did another flip.

They sat there for a while, just holding hands, content to be silent. It was a peaceful scene, Nick thought. The Dobies, seasoned travelers, were sprawled out, drowsing on the other side of his chair.

183

Nick supposed, after last night, he and Amy were all talked out for the moment. They'd covered every subject but one.

He had a wild idea that came right out of left field; a desire that had gotten stronger this afternoon when he'd taken Amy to the site.

He just didn't know how she'd react, so he hadn't brought it up. She liked Chicago so much. So did he. It was her home.

Still . . . a lot of his love for Chicago had been a kind of reaction against the bad old days in Boston. Even his disinterest in sailing was part of that. Once you'd smelled the sea, sailing on a lake wasn't even like sailing.

And standing beside Amy on the wharf that afternoon, smelling the salt smell of the water, his idea looked better than ever.

Nick opened his eyes and looked at her; she was deep in her sketching. He hated to interrupt her right now.

He picked up the report from the table, trying to concentrate on its dry rows of numbers.

Amy's pencil faltered. The sketch was not quite right. She was going in the wrong direction. She couldn't concentrate. Because of that bizarre idea she'd had this afternoon, when they were on the site.

She glanced at Nick. He was immersed in that huge report. This might not be the best time to bring it up.

She started another sketch, but she was still

haunted by the sudden vision that had come to her before.

It was too unlikely, though. Nick must have very bitter memories of Boston, on two counts. Maybe it was better to forget it, let Boston become only a part of their histories.

Still, she couldn't quite let go: during her two brief visits, she'd found so much to love in that city. Boston seemed so solid and so old, a living monument to the past. A place where roots went deep, roots that she had never put down.

But that was absurd. Nick was her roots.

She glanced at him again out of the corner of her eye. He was giving her the same kind of glance.

Then they both spoke, at once.

"Amy, there's something I . . ."

"Nick . . . I was thinking . . ."

They laughed.

"After you," he said.

"No. You first."

"All right. It's that Windom property. That's a damned nice spot . . . overlooking the water."

He *couldn't* be thinking what she'd been thinking. Amy waited.

"You might think I'm nuts, after all that's happened here . . . but you know, a house—"

She spoke right over him. "I was picturing a house there, Nick."

They stared at each other; a wide smile was breaking out on his face.

"A big white house," she said. "With lots of room for whoever else might come along." He grabbed her hand and squeezed it. "And land for the dogs, and maybe some more dogs, and cats. Our own park, not someone else's."

"I don't believe this. I thought about it last night. But I didn't know how to tell you."

"Why not?" Then she answered her own question. "For the same reasons I didn't tell you."

"You thought I couldn't live in the same city with the Windoms, and I thought you couldn't."

She laughed. "It serves us right. There's another thing, Nick . . . the best thing of all."

"I know. It's living on the very land my family was evicted from. That's the biggest payback I could ever make."

"Nick, let's do it."

He raised her hand to his lips, looking very excited. But his eyes were serious and questioning. "Are you up for it . . . are you sure? What about Chicago, Amy?"

And she told him about her feelings for Boston. "Besides, Chicago's not my home. *You* are."

Nick leaned over and kissed her.

Drawing back again, he said, "We've got to be crazy. No one else in America would build a private house on that site."

"We're not like anyone else in America. We never have been and never will be," she retorted.

"I know there's not another one like *you.*"

Holding hands they leaned back in their chairs, preoccupied with plans and happy thoughts.

He was the first to break the silence. "It's the damnedest thing. Something my partner's wife told me, while I was in Washington . . . about what your name means. All this time, and I never knew. She said that Amy means beloved."

She felt the renewed pressure of his fingers.

"As the man said, last November, 'Dearly beloved . . .' "

His voice trailed off. They looked into each other's eyes. She had never seen him look so ecstatic or so sure.

"Dearly beloved," she repeated softly, studying her husband and then their drowsing family of animals . . . the living sculpture more wonderful than anything she would ever devise. "We are gathered here together."

For always, she said in silence. Then she said it aloud.

"For always," he repeated.

This time, it was. And they both knew it.

Sure as May would follow April and the summer turn to fall.

As certain as the sun would rise tomorrow.